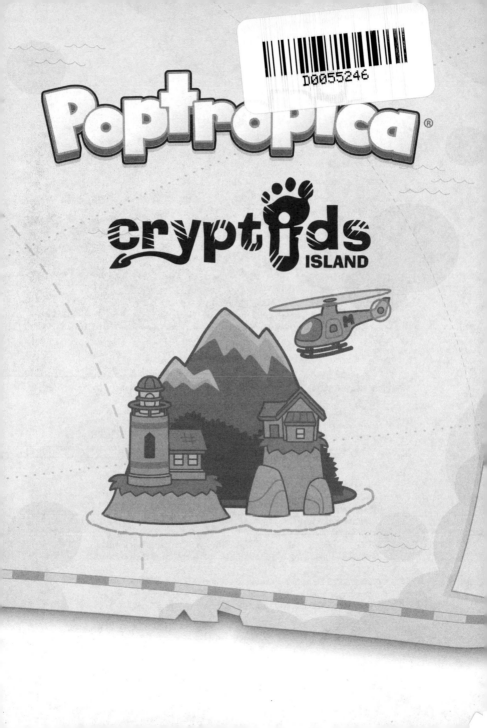

Poptropica®

cryptids ISLAND

POPTROPICA
Published by the Penguin Group
Penguin Group (USA) Inc., 375 Hudson Street, New York, New York 10014, USA

USA | Canada | UK | Ireland | Australia | New Zealand | India | South Africa | China
Penguin Books Ltd, Registered Offices: 80 Strand, London WC2R 0RL, England

For more information about the Penguin Group visit penguin.com

ISBN 978-0-448-46353-7   10 9 8 7 6 5 4 3 2 1

Poptropica®

cryptids ISLAND

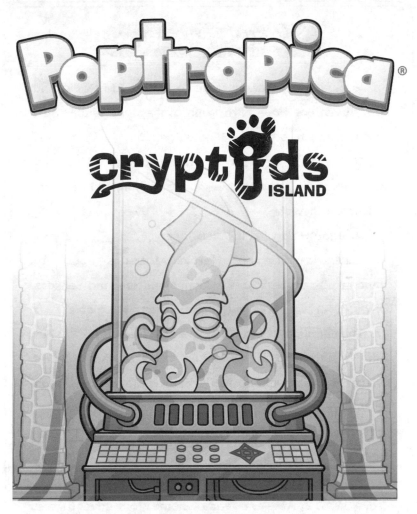

adapted by Max Brallier
cover illustrated by Angel Rodriguez
illustrated by Abraham Evensen Tena
digital render by Nate Greenwall & Nate Tufts

Poptropica
An Imprint of Penguin Group (USA) Inc.

« NEWS FLASH! »

Hey-ya, listeners, welcome to WADV AM Radio and *The Adventure Hour* with your courageous, audacious, and fearless host—me!—Illinois Johnson.

Buccaneers, have I got a scoop for you. This isn't just breaking news—this is smashing, shattering, splintering news!

Are you ready for it? Here goes . . .

Eccentric billionaire Harold Mews is about to announce a contest for "treasure hunters and seekers of fame, fortune, and glory from across the globe."

The details of the contest are as yet undisclosed, but one week from today, all will be revealed! Harold Mews will make the announcement from the Mews mansion in Bucky Cove.

So all you globe-trotting thrill seekers—be there or be left out!

For now, this is Illinois Johnson signing off from WADV AM—the radio home for adventurers, swashbucklers, and thrill seekers!

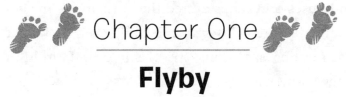

Chapter One

Flyby

Annie Perkins adjusted the propane burner and heard the familiar *whoosh* of flame as the hot-air balloon climbed higher into the sky. She tilted the outboard motor's propeller (that was of her own special design, allowing her perfect control of the balloon), and the balloon picked up speed, moving swiftly through the air, surrounded by nothing but bright blue sky.

Annie checked the height gauge. She was 379 feet up in the sky, but she was as calm and relaxed as if she were lying poolside. Annie was comfortable by herself—she always had been. And that's why she knew she'd go down in history as a legendary adventurer.

"Getting close, now," Annie said aloud.

The small bay town of Bucky Cove was coming into focus. Treetops and the slanted crests of houses and shops dotted the horizon. As the balloon floated closer, Annie could even make out the famous MEWS FOUNDATION sign atop Harold Mews's mansion.

Harold Mews—Annie's hero . . .

It was one week earlier that Annie had made the decision to travel to Bucky Cove and enter the contest. She had been washing dishes at Perkins Dine-In, the small restaurant her family owned. As usual, Annie was listening to WADV AM Radio—it was *The Adventure Hour with Illinois Johnson.* That day, Illinois had broadcast news that grabbed the attention of adventurers across the globe—news about Mr. Harold Mews's million-dollar contest!

Annie could hardly believe her ears. *One million dollars!* Perkins Dine-In was in trouble, and Annie knew that if her family failed to pay back the loans, it wouldn't be long before the bank took away the restaurant. One million dollars would be enough to save it!

Annie told her parents she planned to enter

the contest—but they were *not* having it. "You don't even know what the contest will be!" her mother had exclaimed. "No one does! That Harold Mews is a reclusive nut!"

Annie had just smiled at that, because Annie knew more about Harold Mews than anyone! Since she had been old enough to lift a book, Annie had been reading about Mews's exploits: his journeys deep into the Sahara, his treks across the Andes, his voyages to the North and South Poles.

All his expeditions had the same goal: the discovery of cryptids, strange creatures whose existence has been mentioned, suspected, talked about in hushed whispers—but never truly confirmed by science. Creatures such as Bigfoot, the Loch Ness Monster, or the Atlantic Sea Serpent. Cryptids were Harold Mews's obsession, and they had become Annie's, too.

So, despite her parents' protests, Annie packed her bags, prepared the hot-air balloon, and took to the skies.

She was getting close now, and she saw that she was not the only one drawn to the contest. She had a bird's-eye view of the road leading into Bucky Cove; it was lined with hundreds of vehicles, all approaching the small town.

And it wasn't just cars and trucks! All manner of adventurers in all manner of vehicles were drawn to the contest:

Another hot-air balloon, far in the distance.

A zeppelin, high above her.

An old biplane zooming past her, sputtering and coughing.

Below her, a man in a hang glider swooping and diving.

It would be quite the contest indeed. But Annie had a leg up. She had studied cryptids. She knew where to look and she knew—

Annie's thoughts were interrupted by a high-pitched howl. Annie gripped the side of the basket and spun.

It was a jet! Futuristic and fast. And it was rocketing toward her . . .

"Oh, bananas!"
Annie shrieked as she
furiously adjusted the heat and jerked the
propeller.

"C'mon, c'mon . . . ," Annie said, eyeing the
fast-approaching jet.

With a shrill shriek, the jet blasted past her.
Annie caught a quick glimpse of the pilot: a bug-
eyed woman with bright pink hair interrupted by
a white lightning-bolt-shaped streak. Across the
side of the jet were the words GRIMLOCK GLIDER. The
Grimlock Glider—shiny and silver, with upturned
wings and purple lines—looked like something out

of the old science-fiction magazines Annie loved to read.

"Watch it, ya flying jerk!" Annie shouted.

The jet left a hot trail in its wake, causing an updraft that rocked and tossed Annie's balloon. Next came the downdraft, which forced the balloon toward the ground. Annie cranked the propane heater, but the air currents were too strong. The balloon was out of control and sinking fast.

Annie groaned as she desperately jerked the propeller back and forth. *This adventure is off to a fantastic start . . .*

Annie peeked over the side of the basket. The ground beneath her was growing larger and larger as she spiraled down faster and faster . . .

Chapter Two

The Contest

Mere feet above the road and just seconds before crashing, Annie flung the propeller lever, and the balloon swooped back up, catching a wind current.

Annie might have avoided becoming a splattered splotch on the road, but she wasn't out of the woods yet—in fact, she was heading straight *into* the woods! The balloon was careening toward a small grouping of trees. She needed to get the balloon higher.

She spun the gear on the propane heater, giving it as much gas as it could handle.

Annie looked up. *Incoming tree!*

There was a loud *CRACK!* and then a *WHOOSH!* as the basket clipped the treetops. A leaf with a big bug on it flew into Annie's mouth and—*Yechh!*—she spit it out.

A long plastic banner was strung across the Main Street entrance to Bucky Cove. It read HAROLD MEWS WELCOMES THE WORLD'S GREATEST ADVENTURERS!

With a *rip,* Annie tore right through the banner. The plastic wrapped around her face so that she couldn't see.

"Bananas!" Annie exclaimed.

Thankfully, the wind ripped the banner away—just in time for Annie to see that she was on a collision course with a tall brick chimney poking out of the top of a cute old house.

"Double bananas!" she screamed. She threw the propeller lever again and sent the balloon swinging to the side. The basket scraped against the side of the house. A very round old woman with blue hair in white curlers stuck her fist out the window and called Annie all sorts of names.

"I'm really sorry!" Annie cried out as she swept past.

Annie and her balloon continued spinning and spiraling down Main Street. Annie deftly dodged awnings and trees and flagpoles and TV antennas and satellite dishes and weather vanes and everything else.

Annie squeaked. *Higher! I need to get higher!*

Then—oh no!—Annie spotted electrical lines up ahead, near the Mews mansion. Those would put a very quick, very shocking end to her adventure.

Lower, lower! I need to get lower!

Annie dropped the heat and threw open the vent, forcing the balloon to plummet downward. A rough landing was better than being barbecued!

The balloon slammed into the ground, and the basket crunched and scraped down the street, tossing Annie to the side. She quickly threw an armful of sandbags over the side. When they hit the ground, the whole contraption finally began to slow and then, at last, came to a stop.

Annie gulped in air and let out a huge sigh of relief. "Phew," she said, wiping her brow. "I hope no one saw that!"

And then she looked around.

Oh . . .

Man . . .

Annie had landed *right smack dab in the middle* of the massive crowd of fortune seekers that had gathered at the gates of the Mews mansion in anticipation of the contest announcement.

Everyone stared at Annie: gruff men and stern women, all with wide, judging eyes that said, *"Some adventurer you are! Be gone, young one!"*

Annie felt her face turn bright red. She waved her hand and smiled meekly. "Um, hi, guys. I'm—

ah—I'm here for the contest?"

Thankfully, Annie's embarrassment was short-lived. The gate to the Mews mansion was opening! A hush fell over the crowd.

Is this him? Am I going to see him? Am I finally going to meet my hero?

A figure stepped out from behind the mansion gate. Annie frowned. No, it was not Mews. It was a man with the strict appearance of a butler. The man unrolled a single scroll of paper and loudly hammered it into the mansion's wooden gate.

The huge crowd continued to gather at the gate, all of them clambering to see what the butler had posted. Annie, smaller than all of them, was able to sneak her way through the crowd.

She saw the scroll nailed to the gate. As she read the words, her face lit up.

REWARD
$1,000,000
For irrefutable proof of the
existence of FOUR cryptids.
Search the world and bring your proof to
Harold Mews to claim your reward.
The first to return with proof
will be named the winner!

Annie grinned. She was right! It *was* a cryptid hunt. More than that, it was a *race*!

Murmurs of excitement spread through the thick throng of adventurers. Annie heard the words on their tongues.

"Contest!"

"Cryptid!"

"Race!"

Finally, one of the adventurers called out, "What are we waiting for?! The contest has begun!"

Chapter Three

False Starts and Rough Beginnings

They were off!

Hundreds of adventurers leaped into action, setting off in hopes of finding proof of a cryptid, departing in balloons and boats and helicopters and gyrocopters and big cars and small cars and off-road vehicles and on-road vehicles—everything imaginable!

Annie had hoped to meet Mr. Mews, to talk with him about their mutual love of and belief in the strange creatures classified as cryptids. But to meet him she'd need to win the contest. Annie grinned. *No problemo!*

Annie cranked up the heat, and the balloon lifted into the air. Beneath her, she saw that some other contestants' journeys had already ended:

A bright red hang glider was lodged in a

tree, and its pilot was hanging upside down by a shoelace.

A hot-air balloon not unlike Annie's had landed on a roof and was deflating fast. The owner of the house was out front, swatting at it with a rake.

A woman stood on the side of the road, hands on her hips, looking at her motorcycle as clouds of smoke billowed out of it.

Annie wondered if the same villain—the

woman behind the control stick of the *Grimlock Glider*—had knocked these rivals out of the contest. Annie ignored the thought. *No time to feel sorry for the competition, I've got a contest to win!*

Soon, Annie was soaring past the sandy beaches of Bucky Cove and out over the sea. She inhaled the rich aroma of the Atlantic Ocean and smiled. The adventure had begun.

Annie was heading east to Scotland, in hopes of getting a glimpse—and a photograph—of the most legendary cryptid of them all: the Loch Ness Monster.

Seagulls flapped and squawked, confused at the small girl in the big balloon taking up their airspace. One doofy-looking gull landed on the balloon's ledge.

"Hey there," Annie said to the doofy seagull, smiling. "You coming for the ride?"

The seagull squawked.

"You sure?" Annie asked, laughing to herself. "You're more than welcome to join me!"

The seagull's head cocked to the side, and it looked down to the ocean below. In a flash it flapped its wings and soared away.

"Guess not." Annie shrugged.

A moment later, Annie saw the reason for the gull's sudden departure: There was a speedboat drifting in the water below. It was purple and black with sharp silver lines. Its markings looked to be of the same design as the ones on the jet that had sent Annie spiraling out of control.

Annie floated closer and closer. She saw the words GRIMLOCK GUNNER in bright white on the side—and beside them, an image of a woman with bug eyes and pink-and-white hair.

Bananas! It's her!

Annie watched as the cockpit shifted and slid back, revealing the same woman who had piloted the jet.

"Hello there, girl," the pink-haired woman shouted up to Annie.

Annie scowled and shouted back, "I'm glad to see you down on the water. You shouldn't be allowed in the sky—you nearly killed me!"

The woman laughed—a high-pitched cackle, like a hyena's. "Only nearly? Then I failed."

Annie scowled. *Stupid pink-haired jerk.*

"I'm sorry to be the one to tell you," the pink-haired woman continued, "but that million dollars is mine."

"Well, *I'm* sorry to be the one to tell *you*," Annie shouted back, "but you're in a boat, and I'm up in the sky. So there isn't a whole lot you can do to stop me!"

The pink-haired woman smiled a thin, wicked grin. She leaned forward and pressed a button on the boat's control panel. Suddenly, the back of the boat began to transform. A metal section slid back, there was a mechanical hum, and something began to rise from inside the boat.

It looked an awful lot like a cannon.

"Blast!" Annie exclaimed.

"Sorry to burst your balloon, but I suspect your first adventure will be your last," the woman said, reaching down. She was reaching for something . . . pressing something . . .

Uh-oh.

Suddenly, there was a loud *KA-BOOM* and an eruption of smoke.

"Yikes!" Annie screamed. A flaming cannonball ripped through the balloon. Before Annie knew it—or had time to react or respond— the hot-air balloon was spiraling out of control. She stumbled back. The balloon swept sideways and Annie tumbled out of the basket and through the air.

Annie hit the water with a loud *SMACK!* She rolled her head to the side, just in time to see her balloon plop down into the ocean.

"Enjoy your swim, my dear!" the pink-haired woman shouted as she sped off into the distance.

Annie closed her eyes. What had she gotten herself into? She only wanted to save the family business and, sure, go on a little adventure. Now she was alone, drifting at sea, her only means of transportation destroyed. She shut her eyes. It would be a long swim back to the shore . . .

Suddenly, Annie heard the roar of a very loud engine. The waves became choppy, and gusts of cool air blew over her face, twisting and twirling her wet hair.

Annie's eyes flittered open.

A helicopter?

It was. A helicopter hovered above her. She wasn't imagining things.

It was descending. A ladder was dropping.

On the underbelly of the helicopter, Annie could just make out the words MEWS FOUNDATION.

Annie's eyes closed again.

« NEWS FLASH! »

Hello, listeners, Illinois Johnson here with your daily contest update!

Flawless Frank Gomes was spotted behind the wheel of his *Perfect Peddler* today. Word is, he's on his way to Singapore in search of the Bukit Timah Monkey Man.

Gorgeous Vicki Voyager was just seen high over the Gulf Coast in her hydroplane, headed for the Bahamas to look for proof of that famous flightless bird known as the Chickcharney.

But it's not all good news and great progress! It seems that the treacherous, pink-haired Gretchen Grimlock has already knocked a number of contestants out of the race! The Bandini Brothers were spotted on the side of the road with spikes in their tires—courtesy, Gretchen Grimlock.

One reporter even witnessed Grimlock blast a hot-air balloon out of the sky with a cannonball!

My suggestion? Go home, thrill seekers. Grimlock is in it to win it.

Chapter Four

Believing in the Unbelievable

When Annie came to, she was lying in a giant, supersoft bed. She didn't think she had ever been so comfy in her entire life. She opened her eyes and was happy to see she wasn't staring up at a helicopter, but at a beautiful, ornately tiled ceiling.

It slowly came back to her:

Hot-air balloon.

The contest.

Pink-haired freak!

Cannonball!

And herself—Annie Perkins. Failed adventurer . . .

"You must want that million dollars very badly," a voice said, "to be taking up the chase all alone."

Annie shot up in bed. The voice belonged

to—*she couldn't believe it*—Harold Mews! He was standing at the foot of the bed. She instantly recognized him, clad in his trademark brown fedora, beige suit, and bright red tie. A thin white mustache matched his short white hair.

"Wha—Mr. Mews?" she asked, confused.

He smiled and laughed. "Yes. And you are the young woman who made that most dramatic arrival at my front gate."

Annie's face went red. It wasn't her fault! It was that stupid lady in her stupid jet!

"Oh, no need to be embarrassed!" Harold Mews said. "Your entrance actually reminded me of a trip I once made to the village of Naypyidaw, in Burma. I had just parachuted out of an old triplane with nothing but my canteen, my ferret, Mr. Buckley, and half a chopstick, when—" Mews stopped. "But that's a story for another time." He had a reputation for being a bit long-winded when reciting his exploits, but Annie would have happily listened to them all day long.

Annie scratched her head. "So um—where am I?"

"In my home, of course." Mews chuckled.

"The Mews mansion!" Annie exclaimed.

Mews chuckled again. "Indeed."

"What happened to me?" Annie asked.

"Gretchen Grimlock happened," Mews said, scowling. "I feared her involvement. We pulled you out of the sea in the nick of time."

"That pink-haired woman? That's Gretchen Grimlock?" Annie asked.

Mews nodded grimly.

"She could have killed me!" Annie exclaimed.

"Gretchen is infamous among adventurers—a ruthless fortune hunter. Winning is all that matters to her—and she'll stop at nothing."

Annie shook her head. She was angry at this Gretchen character; but more than that, she was disappointed in herself.

Mews pulled up a chair. "And what about you? As I said, you must want that million dollars quite badly to go it alone."

"Yes," Annie said. "I guess I do. But more than that, well . . ."

Annie stopped. She was going to say something very inspiring and dramatic about how she craved adventure and how she had set out on this journey to prove her mettle and how she wouldn't stop until she had triumphed because she, Annie Perkins, was an adventurer, and she was going to use her adventuring spirit to save the family business. But she felt very silly, all of a sudden. What sort of adventurer was she? She'd made it about one hundred feet and then failed. And what would Mews care about her family's troubles? He was a millionaire. A billionaire!

Bananas, maybe a trillionaire!

"Please continue," Mews said, smiling warmly.

"It's nothing really. Just—I believe in your work. In cryptids. I believe," Annie said, "in the unbelievable."

Mews was silent for a moment. Then he stood and said with a smile, "Very good. When you're done resting, come find me." At the door, he stopped to look back at Annie. "We have work to do."

Three point seven seconds later, Annie was done resting. She threw on her backpack, slipped on her still-soggy sneakers, and left the guest room.

The Mews mansion was amazing! She couldn't believe it! The various artifacts, relics, and ornaments were incredible.

At the end of the hall was a huge grandfather clock with a painting of Bigfoot at the center, the cryptid's arms functioning as clock hands. Outside the bathroom were stuffed dodo birds—*the real*

things! Lining the halls were globes and maps of all sizes and designs. Authentic Greek statues loomed over railings. Hanging on one wall was what appeared to be a *photograph* of a woolly mammoth!

Wow, Annie said to herself as she walked the mansion's long halls. *If I had just1 percent of this, I could support my family for the rest of my life!*

Annie poked her head into room after room. Rooms with dark mahogany floors and leather-bound books. Everything smelled *rich*.

"Excuse me, madam, but where do you think you're going?"

Annie turned, startled. She was looking at Mews's butler—the man she had seen earlier, outside. He looked positively *butler-rific*: tall and thin, dressed in a black tuxedo, wearing white gloves, with a smart little mustache beneath a small nose and tiny round eyes. He appeared to be generally dull and unhappy.

"Sorry, I didn't mean to snoop," Annie said. "I'm looking for Harold Mews. He told me to come find him."

"Oh, yes," the butler said, warming up some. "You must be our guest. Annie Perkins, is that it?"

"Um—yes. But how did you know?" Annie asked, confused.

"Mews knows everything," the butler said. "Please, follow me."

Annie followed the butler down a long hall, through a dark, oak-smelling billiard room, and then down the mansion's wide main staircase into the foyer. It felt like it took about an hour. *This guy moves like molasses on a cold day.*

In the foyer, the butler stopped abruptly beneath what appeared to be a real-deal stuffed Bigfoot.

"Is that—?" Annie began to ask.

"A Bigfoot?" the butler said to Annie.

Annie nodded her head sharply, her eyes wide.

"Just a re-creation. Mr. Mews *wishes* it were real, I suspect. He's obsessed with the things. All a little silly, if you ask me."

Next to the Bigfoot was a very tall and very long bookshelf. Moving slowly and deliberately, the butler took hold of the bookshelf ladder and slid it to the closest end of the bookshelf. Then, again very slowly and deliberately, he climbed the ladder.

Annie was confused. What, this guy decided he just *had* to read some book right now?

At the top of the ladder, the butler leaned over and reached out to grab hold of the Bigfoot's ear. He tugged on it twice. Then, the floor began to rumble, and the massive Bigfoot statue *opened*. It split right down the middle to reveal a dark, winding staircase.

"Oh man. A Bigfoot-ear secret passage?! This is the coolest thing ever!" Annie said. She followed Mr. Butler (that's what she had decided she would call him, until someone told her otherwise) down a dark, cold, winding stairwell. Annie pressed her hands against the cool stone walls to keep from slipping. She felt like she was walking down into a dungeon.

At the end of the spiral staircase was a large metal door. Mr. Butler opened it, and Annie saw then that their destination was not dungeon-like it all. The door revealed a bright room full of buzzing, whirring, and chirping machines. Bright halogen lights hung from the ceiling, and monitors on the wall displayed satellite images from around the world.

At the center of the room was a massive glass tank filled with water. Annie pushed past Mr. Butler and ran to it. Floating in the tank was a cryptid—*a real cryptid.*

"Holy tentacles!" she exclaimed. "It's a giant squid!"

"You know your cryptids," Mews said.

Annie turned to see him watching her from a computer station.

"Of course I do!" Annie said. "I've followed your career my whole life!"

Annie looked around in awe. Mews had assembled small stations devoted to each of the cryptids he hoped to locate: the Loch Ness Monster, the Chupacabra, the Jersey Devil, and more. Annie's eyes were so wide, she thought they'd pop out of her head.

"Welcome," Mews said, with a proud grin, "to the world's only *true* cryptid museum. Now, it's not a museum in the traditional sense, because no one visits it. No one except for me, Mr. Butler, and now you."

"It's—it's—it's all true!" Annie stuttered. "And—wait—your butler's name is Mr. Butler?"

Mr. Butler nodded. Annie suppressed a giggle.

Mews continued. "Thus far we have only one exhibit in this small museum—the body of the giant squid, recovered last week. But it has given me hope that other cryptids exist. That is why I organized this contest."

At the far end of the museum and laboratory was a large workstation, full of displays and monitors. Photos and maps of forests adorned the walls.

"What's that one there?" Annie asked.

"That station," Mews said, "is devoted to my own personal 'white whale,' to borrow a phrase: the North American Bigfoot. It is what drives me. As a small child, younger than you, I *saw* it. I was fishing with my father. I had run off to explore—I was always doing that; the adventurous temperament has been in my blood since birth—and I became lost. Looking for my father, I stumbled upon a cave. Inside was Bigfoot, alone, eating berries. He looked up. He looked me right in the eyes. I turned to call for my father, but when I turned back, the creature was gone."

"Wow," Annie whispered.

"My life changed that day," Mews continued. "I became obsessed. As I grew older, every dollar I made, I put into cryptid research. At last, I was able to build this mansion and this museum and then, finally, hold this contest."

"The contest," Annie said, sighing. "Guess I didn't make it very far, did I?"

"There's still time." Mews smiled.

"Time for what?" Annie asked. "Time to almost get killed again?"

"Time to win," Mews said.

Annie shook her head.

"I won't lie, Annie," Mews continued. "Gretchen Grimlock *will* try to knock you out of the contest again and again. *She's* the real monster. She's the one that deserves to be in a museum—an example of a scientific technique that should be long extinct. That's why I need you, Annie. Did you see them out there? The contestants? Scrambling and fighting. Do you think for one moment they care about these creatures? That they want to see them helped and preserved and cared for? Of course not. They want the money. Nothing more."

"Hey, I'm not allergic to money, either," Annie said. "My family is—"

Mews cut her off. "Don't be silly, of course you're not! And the money will be yours. But you said it yourself: *You believe.* You're not out there just chasing money, you're out there chasing truth— scientific truth! And that's the reason you can win this contest."

Annie sat down on a small metal bench in front of the giant squid's tank. "I can't," she said, shaking her head. "I can't risk my life again."

"Annie, these creatures are out there. And they will be found. Either by Gretchen or by another contestant. The only question is, what will happen to them when they're found? Will they be killed and stuffed and sold? Will they be trapped in a tiny zoo? Or can we help them to live free and safe in their natural habitats?"

Annie thought for a long while about her family. And about Gretchen. Annie had dreamed of adventure her entire life. Dreamed of this moment: of meeting Harold Mews and of seeing actual cryptids.

Now it was here, and she was full of fear. *But fears are meant to be faced!*

Finally, she nodded her head—a quick, hard *yes*. "I'll do it."

Mews clapped his hands and grinned from ear to ear. "Fantastic!"

Chapter Five

Loch and Roll

The Mews Foundation's whirlybird was like nothing Annie had ever seen: a state-of-the-art experimental helicopter with all the trimmings. "No expense spared," Mews boasted.

Mews gave Annie a crash course in flying the whirlybird, although Annie wasn't so sure she loved the term "crash course" when applied to helicopter lessons. She *was* relieved when he showed her the industrial-strength parachute, however.

Annie sat behind the controls and prepared for takeoff. She flicked two green metal switches and the propeller blades began to spin. The whirlybird shook and then there was a roaring, almost deafening sound.

At the center of the flight panel was a monitor that gave Annie direct video-chat access to Mews in the museum. Annie leaned over and pressed a small button, and the monitor flashed on, displaying Mews.

"Oh, Annie, I'm jealous," Mews said. "If I were a younger man, I would join you! Heading off on your first adventure . . . It reminds me of when I was thirteen and I escaped the African village of Korupr by riding a cheetah across a bridge made of elephant hair. I had to fight off a pack of vultures with only a toenail clipper and a gob of toothpaste!"

"Um, Mr. Mews?" Annie said, trying to cut him off before he got going on another one of his stories.

"Right, right," Mews said. "Sorry. Are you ready?"

Annie was scared, no doubt about it. Gretchen Grimlock was out there somewhere, and she'd do anything to keep Annie from winning the contest. Annie pushed the thought out of her mind. "Yep," she said brightly. "Ready as I'll ever be!"

"I've entered the coordinates into your GPS," Mews said, and then asked, "Are you absolutely certain this is the cryptid you want to go after?"

"Positive," Annie replied.

Mews smiled. "Okay, then, good luck. I'll check in when you're close to arrival."

The monitor flashed off.

Annie pulled back on the control stick, the blades spun faster, and the whirlybird lifted off. Soon, the helicopter was cutting through the air, leaving the small town of Bucky Cove behind, passing over the sandy white shore, and then, finally, out over the water. The Atlantic Ocean spread out ahead—far and wide and deep, dark blue all the way to the horizon.

Annie settled in for a long flight.

The sun was setting, and the sky was a deep, creamy orange color when Annie first caught a glimpse of the village of Drumnadrochit. Neighboring the village was Loch Ness. Annie knew from her research that "loch" was the Scottish word for "lake." Thick fog rolled in off the lake and made Drumnadrochit look like something out of a dream.

Mews flashed in over the monitor. "How was your flight?" he asked.

Annie yawned. "Long."

"I once rode a zeppelin from New Zealand to Detroit to Constantinople to Baltimore—all to track down my lucky pants!" Mews said, grinning proudly.

"Um . . . cool?" Annie said.

"Here's the Fact File info on the Loch Ness Monster," Mews continued. "But if you've followed my work as closely as you say, I assume you'll already know most of this."

Mews read the Fact File to Annie:

"'Scotland's Loch Ness receives thousands of visitors each year. They come to catch a glimpse of the legendary monster that is said to swim the loch's deep water. The monster, nicknamed Nessie, is reported to look like a dinosaur with a long neck, flippers, and gray skin like an elephant's.

"'There have been many stories, photos, and even films of Nessie over the years. In the seventh century, a writer named St. Adomnán of Iona told a story about a monk named St. Columba who had chased a strange beast at the River Ness near Loch Ness. In 1933, George Spicer and his wife saw a creature that looked like Nessie cross the road in front of their car, then disappear into the loch.

"'In 1934, a surgeon named Dr. Wilson produced a photo of a long-necked monster. This famous picture convinced many that Nessie was real. Years later a man claimed that he faked the photo using a toy submarine.

"'Since then, many people have taken video evidence of strange humps moving in the water. Researchers and submarines have used sonar to locate any sign of a large beast. Some say that Nessie sleeps in a small body of water off the loch, one that has never been seen by man.

"'Still, Nessie has not been found . . . ,'"

Annie was proud of herself—she had done her research, and none of that information was new to her. She knew no one had ever come close to confirming the creature's existence.

Could she be the first? She wasn't so sure. Mews's Fact File offered little help. And she couldn't very well just dive into the loch and start swimming around trying to find the thing! She'd need to speak with the townsfolk and see what she could learn.

Annie signed off the video chat and set the whirlybird down in a small meadow just outside town. She threw her backpack over her shoulder, shoved her hands into her jacket pockets, and marched through the cool Scottish night. As she made her way along the muddy road, she passed signs proudly boasting of Loch Ness, "the home of ole Nessie." A few shops sold souvenirs, but there were no tourists out now.

Annie threw a glance behind her. She had a gnawing feeling she was being watched. Or worse, followed. She picked up her pace.

A few boats were docked at the edge of town. She'd need a captain, she realized, to take her out on the water. Annie spotted something that was better than any boat: a small submarine, bobbing gently in the water.

That's *exactly* what she needed . . .

Now, to find the submarine's captain.

A great noise erupted from across the street. It came from Nessie's Pub. The laughter, roaring, and cheering grew louder as the door opened and a man walked out.

Annie approached the man and stood up straight, trying to look very grown-up. "What's going on in there?" she asked.

"Y'dun know?" the man said in a thick Scottish accent. "Ole Captain McCullough is throwing darts. Nay a man better in all 'a Scotland."

Annie buttoned up her coat and pushed open the pub's heavy door. *Here goes nothing.*

Inside, it was dark and smoky and crowded and loud. Scottish flags hung from the walls. Annie came up to just about waist-high next to everyone inside. She had never felt smaller in her life. In the back, an old man—Captain McCullough, she assumed—was throwing darts. He held a large drink in one hand that splashed on the floor every time he tossed a dart. A kindly looking gentleman stood behind the bar, watching Annie curiously.

"Ahem," Annie said, pretending to cough into her hand, trying to get the crowd's attention.

It didn't work.

"Ahem!" she said, louder now.

No one turned.

"Hel-lloo!" Annie shouted.

That got them. Everyone stopped what they were doing, heads turned, and the pub went silent. Okay, *now* Annie had never felt so small in her life. She wanted to disappear. But no, she had to press on!

"I'm looking for the captain of the submarine down by the loch," Annie said. "I'd like to commission him to take me in search of Nessie."

Crickets.

"Um. Nessie?" Annie asked. "The Loch Ness Monster? Ring a bell?"

Another moment's silence and the entire bar erupted in laughter. The old man throwing darts, Captain McCullough, turned to look at her. He spoke, silencing everyone. "Aye. That's my sub. And I know where ole Nessie sleeps."

"Great!" Annie exclaimed. "How much to take me?"

"Nothing!" McCullough barked.

Annie beamed. "Oh, great! You'll do it for free? That's so awesome of you—"

"No!" McCullough growled. "I mean nothing 'cause I dona' plan on going! I'll be taking no *girl* like ye."

Again, the pub exploded in laughter.

Annie narrowed her eyes. She stepped forward and reached up, yanking the dart from McCullough's hand. Someone gasped.

"You're pretty good at darts, huh?" Annie said.

"That's right. I'm the best of 'em," McCullough said in his thick Scottish accent.

"You think I'm any good?" Annie asked.

McCullough laughed. "A little girl? Good at darts? No, I dona' think ye would be."

"Well, how about this. If I throw a bull's-eye—one shot only—you take me to get a photograph of Nessie."

No one was laughing now.

McCullough eyed her. "All right," he said, after a moment. "Have at it."

Annie brushed through the crowd and stared down the big round board.

She gripped the cool metal dart tightly.

Her eyes focused on the bull's-eye.

She aimed.

And then she threw . . . .

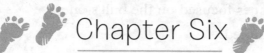

Chapter Six

Into the Loch . . .

Bull's-eye!

"Holy geez," Annie said, her eyes wide. She had nailed it—right in the center! She hadn't expected to even *hit it*. Really, she was really just hoping the captain would think she had guts, gusto, and plucky resolve, enough so he'd agree to help her. But—*BAM!*—she had stuck it good!

Everyone was silent. So silent that, for a moment, Annie could hear the soothing sound of the loch water lapping at the grassy shore outside.

And then came an eruption of cheers!

"Well I'll be . . . ," McCullough said.

Annie smiled proudly.

"All right then," he said. "I'm a man of my word. We'll go as soon as I finish my glass."

"I'll be outside," Annie said. And then, trying

to sound very tough, she finished with, "And I'll be waiting . . ."

Outside, Annie was breathing in the sharp lake air and trying to remain calm. This was it! She was embarking on her first cryptid hunt. She could hardly contain herself. *If only my family could see me now!*

"So you really hope to catch a glimpse, eh?" a voice said. Annie turned. It was the kindly pub keeper, stepping outside.

"Of course," Annie said. "And I don't just *hope* to, I will!"

The pub keeper smiled warmly. "Then take this," he said, handing Annie a metal pennywhistle. "My auld pop used to tell me that if you blow it, Nessie will appear."

Annie smiled and slipped it into her pocket. "Thank you."

McCullough burst through the door. "Let's go, mate!" he said loudly, and began marching down the hill to where the submarine was docked.

Annie waved good-bye to the pub keeper, then ran to catch up. "So you've really seen Nessie?" she asked.

"Sure," McCullough said.

"Have you ever shown her to film crews or tourists or anything?" Annie asked.

"Never," McCullough said.

"But you're going to show me, right?" Annie asked.

"Maybe," McCullough said, with a wide grin.

Annie groaned.

The submarine bobbing beside the dock was very old and very tiny. It appeared that it had once been bright orange, but it was now faded and spotted with rust. It was a testament to Annie's bravery that she only hesitated for about nine minutes before climbing in.

The interior of the ship stunk of mold and something Annie guessed might be frozen pizza topped with wet dog hair. Annie slid into the passenger seat as McCullough plopped down into the captain's chair and began poking at the control panel. McCullough flicked one large switch. The sub coughed and burped, and there was the strong smell of smoke—Annie thought it quite likely that the thing might just roll over and die right there on the spot.

McCullough worked the control stick, which reminded Annie of a joystick straight out of an old arcade machine, and pitched it forward. The sub submerged, diving down into the deep, dark loch. McCullough pulled a lever and one big, bright headlight flashed on.

"Argh, blasted thing," he said, then he pounded the control panel. A second headlight lit up. The crisscrossing beams of light sliced through the murky water. A long striped eel crossed in front of the submarine's thick glass bubble windshield.

"Eww, eels. Gross," Annie said.

"They make for a fine dinner. If ye like, I can catch ye one."

"Eh, I'm good," Annie said.

McCullough snickered as he pitched the stick forward, sending the sub deeper. Annie kept her eyes glued to the depth gauge: 547 feet, 562 feet, 597 feet . . .

At 601 feet, Annie's ears popped for about the twelfth time. "Pretty deep . . . ," Annie said, trying to not sound nervous.

McCullough turned and grinned. "Ya scared yet?"

"No. Are you?" Annie shot back.

McCullough laughed. "It's just a little farther now."

Annie felt butterflies in her stomach. She could hardly believe it. The Loch Ness Monster! She was going to see it! For real! She'd dreamed about this moment—the actual sighting of a cryptid—for as long as she could remember. And now it was about to happen!

But then she remembered something . . . It *was* called the Loch Ness *Monster*. Not the Loch Ness Teddy Bear or the Loch Ness Cuddly Sue. The Loch Ness *Monster* . . .

"Hey," Annie asked. "It's not—um—it's not going to, like, eat the sub or anything, right?"

"What, ole Nessie?" McCullough laughed.

"No, no. A pussycat, she is."

"Okay," Annie said, not quite convinced.

The water turned darker still as the ship dove deeper. Annie eyed the gauge again: 732 feet deep . . .

McCullough pulled a lever, there was a loud clanking, and the sub began gently drifting through the water. McCullough flicked a switch and the headlights went doubly bright. A school of salmon dispersed. Through the scattering fish and the gently swaying lake plants, a large object came into focus.

"There she is," McCullough said, pointing. "Ole Nessie."

Annie leaned forward on the control panel and squinted. She could make out a large figure with a very fat, very round body and a long, extended neck. But even with the help of the submarine's headlights, it was hard to see exactly what was what.

"Get closer," Annie whispered.

"I can't," McCullough said. "It's too dangerous. Ye'll have to snap your photo from here."

51

"I can't see anything! You promised me you'd show me Nessie, and we're not going anywhere until I see Nessie. Closer!"

McCullough muttered something, but he did as he was asked and pushed the stick forward.

Annie watched with bated breath. She saw eyes. A mouth. Scaly skin.

It's real . . .

She could hardly contain herself.

But—

She also saw what looked like rust. And was that? Words on the side? Yes . . . GREAT SCOT FILM GROUP.

Hmm . . .

"Hey!" Annie said, suddenly realizing the truth. "That's not the Loch Ness Monster! That's just a busted old movie prop!"

McCullough's face went red. "Aye. It was from a horror film titled *Nessie: Scotland's Original Scream Queen*. Quite scary, I thought."

Annie glared at him. "You're trying to put one over on me."

McCullough shrugged.

"We had a deal. I want to see the real Nessie," Annie said, "*now.*"

McCullough waved her off. "Ye think I know where Nessie is? Of course not!"

Annie's heart sank. She glared at the captain.

"Let me out!" Annie said, finally.

"What?"

"You scammed me! If you're not going to show me where Nessie is, I'll find her myself!"

"No, no. I can't do that," McCullough said. "Yer just a little girl—ye can't be out here all alone. I'll take ye back to the shore."

Annie leaned over and looked very serious. "I said *let me out.*"

McCullough frowned, but did as she asked. He pulled back on the stick, and a minute later, the ship was surfacing. It was dark except for the moon above when the little submarine emerged at the southern edge of Loch Ness. The hatch clanged open, and Annie climbed out. McCullough followed. He looked around. "I don't even know where we are," he said, scratching his head.

Annie didn't care. She was too furious. Not finding the creature was one thing, but she had been duped like a sucker! That was ten times worse!

Annie jumped off the submarine and landed on the muddy, mucky shore.

"Ye can't just go wandering around trying to find Nessie!" McCullough shouted.

"Oh yeah?" Annie shouted. "Watch me!" Then she turned her back to McCullough and marched into the dark night.

Chapter Seven

Two Blows on the Whistle

Annie walked along the shore for hours. Her legs were tired, and her heavy backpack made her shoulders sore. She replayed the Fact File in her head, trying to recall some clue that might help her find what no one else had. The Fact File had said, "Some say that Nessie sleeps in a small body of water off the loch, one that has never been seen by man." But Annie saw no body of water connected to the loch.

A chill blew off the water. Annie buttoned up her coat. She felt so far from home . . . Trying to stay warm, she stuck her hands into her pockets. She felt something cold. *The pennywhistle!* She pulled it out.

There were words engraved on the whistle! How had she missed them before? Annie held the whistle up to her eyes and squinted.

When dawn is upon ye, and the water is low
Only then will Nessie finally show

At that very moment, warmth washed over Annie. The sun was coming up over the distant mountains, and bright rays of light shone down on her. It was morning! Annie hadn't realized how long she had been walking on the shore.

When dawn is upon ye . . .

"Well, it is!" Annie exclaimed.

Annie squinted and peered out at the lake. She spotted the tide marker jutting high out of the water. The water was low!

Everything was lining up. But what did it mean?

The answer, Annie realized, was right beneath her! She was standing in a streambed—but there was no stream! When the tide was low, the stream was just a muddy path. A bright ray of sunlight lit it up.

Annie waded along the path. She was walking *down*. The path was actually the entrance to a very small and very narrow canyon! The streambed ramped farther downward. With both the tide low

and the sun at its current position, something was
visible . . .

An entryway!

Annie's feet splashed in the wet mud as she
ran toward the opening.

She found herself in a pitch-black tunnel. The
streambed at her feet and the tunnel around her
grew wider and deeper and murkier. There was
water in the tunnel, and it was soon up to Annie's
waist. She began swimming.

*This is no stream. It's a full-blown river, and it's
underground!*

The dark tunnel wound around a corner.
Annie glimpsed a small light at the end. She swam
faster—she was close! She could feel it!

Finally, she came out of the tunnel. She was
soaking wet and exhausted. She crawled up onto
the shore.

And there, entirely hidden beneath tall,
overhanging trees, was a small lake.

Whoa.

"Whoever would have thought that tunnel
would lead to this?" Annie said. The water was

calm and quiet and serene. She wondered when the last time a person had been here was—it looked completely untouched by human hands.

But there was no Loch Ness Monster.

The pennywhistle!

Annie pulled it from her pocket, whipped it around to dry it out, and then lifted it to her lips.

Here goes nothing.

She blew twice—hard and sharp. The shrill sound cut through the quiet morning air.

Nothing happened.

She waited a moment, holding her breath—hoping—but still, nothing . . .

"I don't believe it!" she cried out. "I would have sworn this was it! It felt like I was—"

Annie stopped. She squinted and looked out at the water. Something was happening. The water was being drawn to the center of the lake, like someone had yanked the plug from a drain. And then, suddenly, it reversed! Water began rushing out from the center of the lake, out toward the small shore where Annie stood. Water splashed up over her sneakers.

And then it—*she*—appeared.

Nessie. The Loch Ness Monster.

She began to rise up out of the water.

Nessie looked very old. She was green and gray, with a face like some kind of dinosaur. Strings of pond scum hung from her mouth.

She looked out at Annie through thin, lizard-like eyes.

Annie was suddenly very scared. *Don't eat me, don't eat me, don't eat me . . .*

But then the big beast smiled and blew a stream of water at Annie, soaking her.

Annie laughed. *Aww, it's sweet!*

Very slowly, keeping one eye on the massive cryptid the entire time, Annie reached into her bag and pulled out her waterproof camera. Her finger found the

shutter button and
she snapped a photo.

KA-KLICK!

Seconds later,
Mews's state-of-the-art
camera spit out a photo.
Instant proof!

Annie then sat with her
back to a tree and rested for a
short while, enjoying the peace
and quiet and the view of a creature that she had
dreamed about her entire life.

She had done it.

She had found her first cryptid.

And she had proof.

Or not . . .

There was a sudden roar above Annie. A
helicopter was chopping through the sky, just
barely visible through the towering, leafy trees.

"Gretchen!" Annie said.

The mechanical roar of the helicopter
frightened Nessie, and the animal splashed in the
water. Annie watched Nessie dive and disappear

beneath the surface.

When Annie looked back up, there was a boot in her face! Gretchen, rappelling down a rope through the trees, was upon her!

Gretchen landed right on Annie's head—*bonk!*—and sent her stumbling back.

"Thank you, my dear," Gretchen said, and yanked Annie's photo out of her hands.

"Hey, that's *my proof*!" Annie cried.

"I'm afraid it's mine now," Gretchen said with an evil grin. Annie ran toward the villain, but Gretchen tugged on the rope, and in a split second she was yanked back up to the helicopter. Annie could do nothing but watch her go . . .

« NEWS FLASH! »

Howdy, listeners! Illinois Johnson here with an update on Harold Mews's cryptid contest.

The daredevil fortune hunter Ervin "the Machine" Makow took his souped-up motorcycle to Wisconsin in search of the cryptid known as the Goat Man, but he was forced off the road by a freak storm. That was two days ago, and it's still raining! Some suspect that Gretchen Grimlock is using her infamous TTT—Targeted Thunderstorm Technology—to keep the Machine sidelined.

Meanwhile, Flawless Frank Gomes successfully made it to Africa—but is now trapped in a tar pit! A sticky situation, indeed.

But the real news is young Annie Perkins and her back-and-forth battle with Gretchen Grimlock. Everyone's favorite young cryptid chaser was onto something BIG: authentic photographic evidence of that famous Loch Ness lake monster, Nessie—but Gretchen ripped the proof right out of her hands!

We'll be back with more contest news as soon as we get it. Don't touch that dial, adventure fans!

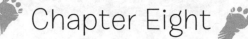

Chapter Eight

The Goat Sucker

"I had it!" Annie exclaimed. "I had a *real* photo of the *real* Loch Ness Monster. And Gretchen stole it!"

Annie was behind the control stick of the whirlybird, flying low over the Scottish coastline. On the video monitor, Mews frowned.

"You must press on," Mews said. "I never said it would be easy. You know, the whole situation reminds me of some work I did on an island for a strange doctor named H. G. I had completed my work, but he took credit and tried to feed me to a puma! I barely escaped—had to build a raft out of banana peels! And by the time—"

"Mr. Mews!" Annie exclaimed. "We don't have much time!"

"Right, sorry," Mews said. "Tell me, Annie, what do you know of the Chupacabra?"

Annie gulped. The Loch Ness Monster was a gentle beast—every report had said so. But the Chupacabra? That was, like, a for-real *monster*. "Um, I know it's scary," Annie said. "Like creepy carnival-clown scary."

"Here's what the Fact File says," Mews said, and began reading:

"'In 1995, several Puerto Rican farmers were faced with a strange puzzle. The goats and chickens on their farms had died mysteriously during the night. The animals had two puncture wounds in them, almost like marks from a vampire's fangs. Was a coyote to blame? A panther? Wild dogs? The villagers didn't think so. They were sure that the creature that had attacked their animals was a Chupacabra, Spanish for "goat, sucker."

"'Although the first Chupacabra sighting was reported in 1950, after the 1995 sightings Chupacabra fever swept the world. As reports came in, people started sketching what they thought the beast looked like: about five feet tall with a large mouth full of sharp fangs. It had large, red, alien-like eyes, stood on two legs, and had very sharp claws.

"'Some people have taken pictures of what they believe are dead Chupacabras, but scientists have proven that those photos show only coyotes with a disease called mange. Does this prove that the Chupacabra doesn't exist? Nobody has yet explained how all those goats and chickens died. And those who have seen the Chupacabra have said they'll never forget the monster with the glowing eyes . . .'"

"Sounds like a grand old time," Annie said nervously.

"Set your coordinates for Puerto Rico," Mews replied.

"Mr. Mews, one question," Annie said, just as Mews was about to sign off.

"Yes, Annie?" he asked.

"Gretchen knew I would be at Loch Ness. She knew *exactly* where I was going to be and *exactly* when I'd be getting there. How is that possible?"

Mr. Mews fiddled with his mustache as he thought. "I can't say for sure. She has a network of operatives. Also, that radio host sure blabbers a lot."

Annie nodded.

"Check in once you've arrived," Mr. Mews said. Then he signed off.

A few button presses later and the whirlybird was banking away from the Scottish coastline and soaring out over the vast expanse of white-capped waves that was the Atlantic Ocean. Annie flipped the switch marked AUTOPILOT. She leaned back, closed her eyes, and was soon fast asleep—dreaming alternately of a horrible monster with glowing eyes and a million-dollar payday that would save her family from bankruptcy.

The heat was stifling. It was now early morning, and Annie was marching across Puerto Rican farmland in search of the infamous Chupacabra. The breeze coming off the rolling grassy hills did little to cool the air.

"Hey, you there, halt!" a voice shouted. Annie spun. The voice belonged to a farmer. He was marching up the hill behind Annie, holding on to a pitchfork like he planned on poking a few holes in her with it.

"You a human being?" he asked sharply.

"Huh?" Annie said, confused.

"You're not, *y'know*," the farmer said, looking around nervously like someone might be listening, "El Chupacabra."

Annie laughed. "No, I'm not the Chupacabra."

The farmer smiled. He was a large man— nearly seven feet tall, Annie guessed. But he reached into his pocket and pulled out the *tiniest* pair of glasses Annie had ever seen. He slipped them onto his nose, and Annie couldn't help but giggle.

"Oh yes," the farmer said. "You're clearly a person. I see that now."

"I *am* on the hunt for the Chupacabra, though," Annie said. "Do you know anything about it?"

"Know anything about it?!" the farmer exclaimed. "It is my archenemy!"

"What do you mean?" Annie asked.

"Chupacabra is ruining my life! Harassing my animals. It ate two of my goats!"

"Then we'll just have to catch it, won't we?" Annie said, with a sly grin.

The farmer's name was Felix Aviles, and he lived in a beautiful, Spanish-style farmhouse that stood at the center of a sprawling ranch. He gave Annie a short tour, showing her the cows and goats that grazed the fields and the large plantain trees that towered over the property. They walked the length of his farm. Annie wasn't quite sure what she hoped to find, but she figured she'd know it when she saw it.

And she did, just moments later.

But before she saw it, she tripped over it.

She hit the ground, rolled end over end, then sat up rubbing her head. She had tripped on the skeleton of a goat. She looked closer. On the bones, she saw thick, deep tooth marks.

Whatever ate this poor goat was awful hungry.

"See?!" Felix said, helping Annie to her feet. "Goat bone! Dang Chupacabra ate that goat! Please find that monster!"

Annie frowned. *Easier said than done.* No dart games to help her here. Annie ran her hand through her hair, thinking . . .

"Has anyone ever had any luck?"

"No," Felix said.

"Is there a place where the creature has been spotted? Where we could look?" Annie asked.

"There is one place . . ."

"Where?" Annie asked excitedly.

"You can't go. It's too dangerous!"

"I'll decide if it's too dangerous. Where?"

"In the mountains, there is a place known as the Devil's Jaw. Many goat bones have been found there. Some suspect it's where the animal feeds."

Annie smiled. "Then what are we waiting for?"

It was a long, treacherous trip. Felix drove his old pickup truck up along the tree-lined mountain paths. "Does anyone ever come up here?" Annie asked.

Felix shook his head. "Many have come to the island in search of El Chupacabra. But few have come up here—the danger is too great."

After a long day's journey, they came to the strange collection of boulders and stones known as the Devil's Jaw. Large rocks jutted out of the ground like fangs. Through the rock fangs was a small clearing surrounded by high stone walls. There was only one way in and one way out. Inside the rocky hideaway were piles and piles of goat bones. It was a ghastly sight and it seemed clear to Annie that this was, indeed, the Chupacabra's feeding spot.

Now what? Knowing where the cryptid fed was one thing. Catching it was another thing entirely! Annie looked around, searching for a clue to how they might actually catch the creature. "I have no idea what to do," Annie said after a moment, frustrated. "Bananas!"

"No, no, not bananas. They're called plantains," Felix said. "They're like Puerto Rican bananas."

Annie looked at Felix, confused—then she realized what he meant. Large plantain trees were towering over them, and the plantain fruit *did* look an awful lot like bananas. "Oh, I didn't mean bananas, like the fruit," Annie said. "'Bananas' is just sort of something I say sometimes when I'm frustrated or annoyed or scared or hungry or pretty much anytime really."

"Oh. Okay . . . ," Felix said. Annie figured he probably thought *she* was bananas.

Annie was still looking at the tree when a large, ripe plantain fell to the ground. And very quickly, a small rodent scurried from the underbrush, pounced on the plantain, and dragged it away.

Annie smiled. She had an idea . . .

Minutes later,
Annie was behind
the wheel of Felix's old
pickup truck, driving with serious
speed. The speakers were blasting
Puerto Rican calypso and Annie couldn't help
but smile: She was so far from home—so far from
what she'd known her whole life—and she was in
the midst of an adventure for the ages!

Annie gunned the engine, and it barked and
roared as she raced down the mountainside. She
kept her eyes glued to the path ahead—waiting,
hoping, and then . . .

A goat sprinted out from behind a rock up
ahead.

"There you are!" Annie exclaimed.

She sped up, staying behind the animal. The goat leaped over a small rock formation. Annie cut the wheel hard and careened around the rock, barely staying on the path. She came up behind the goat, blasting the horn.

The animal turned its head and looked at her like she was absolutely insane.

"Sorry, goat!" Annie shouted over the roar of the engine. "I just need to borrow you for a sec!"

She turned hard toward the bounding animal, the truck's cab bouncing like crazy. The goat made a loud goat noise—something like *MAAAA!!!!*—and then it hooked to the right and took off in the other direction, back up the mountainside.

"Good," Annie said, watching the goat run. "Thataway."

The goat began to sprint to the left, but Annie floored it and the truck lurched ahead, pulling alongside the goat and herding it back to the right. She kept her foot on the gas, guiding the animal forward. A second later, Annie slowed down as the goat sprinted through the narrow entrance to the Devil's Jaw.

Perfect.

Annie parked the truck. She took a long drink of water, then walked past the large stones and into the Devil's Jaw. Felix was waiting for her on the other side.

"Over here!" Felix shouted from behind a boulder. "The trap is all set!"

Felix had tied the mountain goat to a tree with a thick rope. Just in front of the goat was a huge wooden crate. A stick held the crate up off the ground. As soon as the Chupacabra got close enough to bump the stick . . . *BAM!* The crate would drop, and they'd have the Chupacabra caught!

Now there was nothing to do but wait.

Annie followed Felix's lead and ducked behind the boulder.

"You think it'll work?" Felix asked, adjusting his glasses.

"I hope so!" Annie said.

They waited and waited and waited. Annie

wondered if she had been wrong. Had her trap been silly? Maybe this wasn't even where the Chupacabra fed. Maybe the creature didn't even exist!

No. Don't think that way. It's like I told Mews. I believe in the unbelievable.

And then, at that moment, she heard a loud snap. Annie peered around the boulder. The trap had been sprung: The wooden crate had dropped and the mountain goat stood safely beneath the tree. Etched on the goat's face, however, was a look of sheer terror. Annie stepped close to the animal, running her hand over its short, coarse hair, soothing it.

And then she turned to the crate.

Inside that crate, Annie hoped, would be the Chupacabra.

Annie crept toward the box. She heard movement inside it. Scraping.

The sounds of the Chupacabra?

Annie crept closer still. There was banging from inside the box now. Annie's heart pounded in her chest. She placed her ear to the box and . . .

Chapter Nine

All Fed Up

The box was tossed into the air and thrown aside! Annie pulled her hand away and leaped back, terrified. "The Chupacabra is loose!" she shouted.

"Plantains!" Felix screamed as he dove back behind the rock.

But it was *not* the Chupacabra.

It was Gretchen Grimlock!

The villain stood where the box had been. Her long pink hair whipped around in the wind.

"Gretchen!" Annie exclaimed.

"You terrible little girl," Gretchen snarled. "What are you doing here?"

"I followed you in hopes of catching the Chupacabra. I never thought I'd fall into your inane little trap!"

"Followed me how?!" Annie exclaimed. "I

didn't see anyone behind me!"

"That's my little secret," Gretchen said, winking.

Annie's eyes went wide. Her jaw hung open. A look of terror flashed across her face.

"That's right," Gretchen said, seeing the expression on Annie's face. "You're scared. Good! You *should* be scared. Because I am TERRIFYING!"

"Gretchen. Be-be-behind you," Annie stuttered.

Gretchen put her hands on her hips. "I'm not falling for that one." She scowled.

"Chu—Chu—" Annie stuttered, her eyes wide.

"Oh, look at you—you're so scared that you've completely lost your mind! You're imitating a train conductor! Choo-choo!" Gretchen howled. "Choo-choo!"

"Chu—Chu—*Chupacabra*!" Annie screamed.

"Huh?" Gretchen said, finally turning. And then she saw it, too . . .

The Chupacabra loomed at the entrance to the Devil's Jaw. It was a vicious, howling, growling monster. It looked like a large, mangy dog—but with gray, almost blue skin. Small bony spikes protruded from its body.

What Annie noticed most were its eyes: two small glowing red dots. Those eyes seemed to lock on to Annie, ignoring everything else. Those eyes were the most horrifying things Annie had ever seen.

Annie stepped back, ready to run. But where? There was nothing but jagged rock surrounding them—the only way in and out was through the entrance, and the Chupacabra stood in front of that. The cryptid stepped forward. It snarled and shook its head, spraying white spittle.

And it kept its eyes locked on Annie.

Suddenly, Annie felt something. The ground was shaking beneath her feet. Ahead of her, two mountain goats charged through the entrance. The Chupacabra turned its ugly head just as another goat entered. And another. In an instant, there were a dozen goats charging—a full-on stampede!

The first goat collided with the Chupacabra,

hitting it directly in the jaw. The beast's head snapped back. It yelped, and then it began running. Now the entire stampede—with the Chupacabra out front—was coming straight for Annie.

"Bananas!" Annie yelped.

She looked around frantically. Nowhere to run and nowhere to hide. But maybe . . . yes! Above her was the plantain tree. Her only option. She leaped up and grabbed hold of the lowest leaf.

The Chupacabra was closing in on her, charging and roaring. Annie lifted her feet just as it charged beneath her—she felt its thick, bristly hair against her ankles as it passed. As she clung on for dear life, Annie saw Gretchen in the distance, escaping through the now-clear entrance. *Argh!*

The goats chased the Chupacabra around the rock enclosure and then back through the entrance.

The creature was gone.

Phew!

Just as quickly as it had begun, it was over. Annie dropped to the ground and dusted herself off.

"Close one," Felix said as he came around from behind the boulder.

"Hopefully it'll leave your animals alone now," Annie said. "At least for a while."

"I hope so," Felix said.

Annie looked up at the sun and squinted. So the Chupacabra was real. And the trap would have worked. But Gretchen Grimlock had gotten in the way. Annie had gotten nothing, nothing for all her—

Suddenly, out the corner of her eye, she noticed something flashing!

Annie ran over. A tooth! A Chupacabra tooth! Annie picked it up and grinned. "Nice try, Gretchen," Annie said, "but in the end, *I* got the proof."

Annie and Felix drove back down the mountain. If she was going to get more proof, Annie needed to do something about Gretchen. She'd never win the contest with someone out there plotting and scheming and cheating and battling her at every moment. Next time, Annie swore, she'd be ready for Gretchen.

Back in the helicopter, Annie flipped on the monitor and called Mews.

"Mr. Mews," Annie said. "I've got a plan. I want you to call up Illinois Johnson at WADV Radio and tell him that I'm traveling to New Jersey to look for the Jersey Devil."

Mr. Mews was confused. "But why?"

"Because he'll announce it on the radio, and Gretchen will follow. And I'll be waiting for her. I'm going to knock her out of this contest."

Mr. Mews smiled. "How devious! Reminds me of the time . . ."

« NEWS FLASH! »

Adventure update! Illinois Johnson at WADV, *The Adventure Hour*, here with the latest on Harold Mews's cryptid contest!

Brilliant inventor I. P. Lawe was headed to West Africa to track down the jungle walrus (that's right, a walrus that lives in the jungle!) known as the Dingonek, but he was sidetracked by sabotage! At five thousand feet, the wings fell off his plane! Good thing he thought to invent the world's greatest parachute! My guess at the saboteur? All I'll say is, it rhymes with Fetchen Fimsock . . .

I've just received word that Annie Perkins, after nearly nabbing the Chupacabra in Puerto Rico, is now on her way to New Jersey to hunt for the infamous Jersey Devil. And we're not talking hockey here—we're talking winged monsters!

Happy hunting, contestants! And now, a word from our sponsors . . .

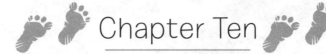

Chapter Ten

Net Gains

Two days later, Annie walked into the Ticktock Diner in Leeds Point, New Jersey. Using information provided by Mr. Mews, Annie had tracked the cryptid known as the Jersey Devil to this small town. Legend said the creature haunted an old house on Prescott Road.

"Excuse me, I'm looking for this road," Annie said to the waitress behind the counter as she unfolded her map. "Do you know how to get there?"

The waitress smiled warmly and drew directions to the road on the map.

"Thanks so much," Annie said.

"Sure, happy to help," the waitress said, smiling. "You be careful!"

But as soon as Annie walked outside, the waitress pulled a walkie-talkie from beneath the counter . . .

"Ms. Grimlock," the waitress said into the walkie-talkie, "you were right. The girl was here. She's headed out to the old Prescott place now. Good luck."

Outside, Annie examined her surroundings. She felt like she was being watched . . . followed . . .

Good. Come and get me, Gretchen. Walk right into the trap I've set.

Prescott Road was long, narrow, and lined with massive oak trees. Annie raced along atop a small yellow dirt bike. Its bright halogen headlight cut through the night and lit up the trees. She navigated the road's dark twists and turns as best she could, slowing down when necessary to avoid careening off into the woods.

As she rode, she kept her eyes on the rearview mirror. She was waiting for Gretchen to appear and, once again, try to knock her out of the contest.

As Annie rode, her mind wandered to the cryptid she was chasing. Eyes glued to the road and hands tight on the handlebars, Annie recounted Mews's Fact File on the Jersey Devil:

"'It started three hundred years ago in the Pine Barrens of New Jersey. On a dark, moonless night Mother Leeds gave birth to her thirteenth child. A hideous creature emerged, with leathery wings, a long tail, horns, and a head like a horse. It let out a terrible cry and flew up the chimney.

"'Since then, many sightings of the creature have been recorded. An early report came from naval commodore Stephen Decatur in the 1800s. He saw the beast flying across the sky. He shot a cannonball at it, but the Jersey Devil kept flying.

"'In 1909 there was a rash of sightings. In one town the beast flew around a trolley full of people. One witness found hoofprints on a roof. Another woman heard a noise in her yard and went outside to see the Jersey Devil holding her dog. She hit the creature with a broom, and it dropped her dog and flew away.

"'Skeptics think the Jersey Devil is a large bird, such as the great horned owl. In recent years there haven't been as many sightings, but people still report hearing its unearthly cry in the woods late at night.'"

The roar of an engine snapped Annie's focus

back to the mission at hand. Behind her was a motorcycle, catching up fast. *Gretchen* . . .

Annie's bike was jolted by a hard hit from behind. Gretchen cackled. Annie did her best to maintain a grip on the bike's handles as the road twisted and turned. It grew darker as they raced deeper into the woods.

Soon, she'd be upon the trap: a net strung across the road that would entangle Gretchen.

Annie narrowed her eyes, scanning the road ahead.

There!

Annie *slammed* on the brakes, and Gretchen rocketed past her—straight into the net!

Annie's trap had worked! Gretchen was instantly yanked off her motorcycle and entangled in the net. The motorcycle rocketed off into the woods, leaving Gretchen strung up like some unlucky bug caught in a spider's web.

Annie climbed off her bike.

"You rotten little thing!" Gretchen howled.

"Me?" Annie exclaimed. "You shot me out of the sky! You scared away the Loch Ness Monster! I almost got eaten by the Chupacabra because of you!"

Gretchen glared.

Annie reached her hand inside Gretchen's coat pocket and snatched the photo of the Loch Ness Monster. "Now I have my proof back!"

Gretchen glared *harder*. "You'll never win!"

Annie stepped away from the dangling villain and flipped on her Mews Foundation communicator. "Mr. Mews, it went exactly as planned!"

"Fantastic!"

"And I got the photo back!"

"Wonderful. Only two more to go and the contest is yours!"

Annie didn't respond. Something in the distance had caught her attention: a rundown old house, alone in a field.

"Annie, are you there?" Mews said.

"Yes, I'm here. And I believe I'm looking at the house of the Jersey Devil . . ."

"Annie, be careful."

"I will," Annie said.

She shut off the Mews Foundation communicator and approached the dark house. All the while, Gretchen kept howling at her.

Chapter Eleven

The House of the Jersey Devil

"I must be clinically insane," Annie said to herself as she crept toward the house. It was nearly pitch-black now, and even the crickets had stopped chirping.

She grabbed hold of the old door handle. It felt strangely warm. Without even being pushed, the door swung open and made a long, chilling, creaking sound.

Inside, moonlight shone through the windows, casting eerie rectangles of light on the floor. A cool draft blew through the house, and a chandelier swayed lightly in the breeze.

Annie gently swung her backpack off her shoulder and reached inside for her flashlight. She flicked it on. What she saw made her blood run cold.

It was the horrid and disfigured face of
an elderly man! The man had no eyes—just
holes where they should have been. Red streaks
were visible on his face. Annie shrieked and the
flashlight clanged to the floor.

It took Annie a moment to realize that it
was only a painting. A very old, very creepy
painting—one only a total *nut job* would hang in
their house—but still, just a painting. Vandals had
splashed it with paint and sliced it apart.

Get it together, Annie, she said to herself.

She picked up the flashlight and proceeded
to explore the bottom floor of the house. The
floorboards creaked with every step, and a thick
layer of dust covered everything. Mice skittered
across the floor and thick cobwebs filled the
doorways. But beyond that, there was nothing of
interest on the first floor. And no signs of the giant
winged creature known as the Jersey Devil.

"Upstairs we go, then," Annie said aloud.

The stairs were old and rotten, so Annie
walked slowly and carefully. She didn't want to
fall through and be trapped in the basement—it

was probably nightmare central down there.

The second floor of the house was no better than the first. Bedrooms that still held beds, dressers, and nightstands. Old newspapers tacked to the wall—some hung loose and swayed in the breeze. *Creeptown, USA.* But no sign of any monster.

"Well, that's it, I guess . . . ," Annie said, partially relieved. "I struck out."

Walking back down the stairs, Annie felt a cool chill blowing over the creaky old staircase steps and up her leg. Annie slowed down and took every step carefully. The last thing she wanted was to—

Crack!

One floorboard snapped.

Uh-oh.

Annie took another careful step—and another floorboard cracked. Annie's foot burst through.

Oh no.

Annie lunged for the staircase railing just as two more floorboards cracked. Wood splintered, Annie slipped, and she fell *through the staircase!*

A long moment later, Annie landed on her butt, *hard*. She was sprawled out on the cool dirt basement floor. But she could see nothing. It was pitch-black. She reached around for her flashlight, searching in the darkness.

She could hear herself breathing. She slowed her breath. She had to calm down.

But she could *still* hear herself breathing. Unless . . . ? Unless that wasn't Annie breathing . . .

Annie felt around for her flashlight. She found it, flicked it on, and—

"*SCAHHH!*"

"Ahhh!" Annie screamed. She was staring at a terrible, horrible, freaky horse face! The face of the Jersey Devil! The creature filled the entire basement.

Annie frantically looked for an exit, but there was none. This basement had no doors! No wonder no one had ever found the Jersey Devil before—only Annie's fall had revealed the creature!

The horrific cryptid moved toward her.

Annie's heart pounded. She looked up. She could climb back out of the basement, but she needed to buy some time . . .

Her camera!

She ripped it from her bag and fumbled for the ON button. After what felt like an eternity, she found it and—*click*—snapped a photo. The bright white flash lit up the room and blinded the Jersey Devil. It reeled back, holding one of its huge, disgusting wings over its eyes.

"*SKEEE!*" The cryptid howled, then turned and scampered toward a fireplace in the corner. Somehow, it wormed its way inside, and with a *whoosh*, it flew up the chimney!

Annie breathed the world's biggest sigh of relief. *It's gone!*

As quickly as she could, Annie climbed the wall to the broken staircase then crawled up onto the first floor. She needed to get out of this house, now! Her legs went into overdrive, and she sprinted out through the front door and into the night.

She heard the flapping of wings behind her. It was a disgusting, almost wet sound. She kept running. A tree jutted out of the ground not far from the house, and Annie ducked behind it. After a moment, she calmed down. Sweat was still pouring off her face, and her heart was still pounding, but she wasn't about to pee her pants—so that was good. She peeked around the side of the tree. Next to the house, the devil was flapping its huge wings and preparing to fly away.

Annie breathed a long sigh of relief. *I'm safe. I'm going to be all right.*

But then another thought entered Annie's mind—a thought more frightening than the Jersey Devil itself: *I'm a wuss! I had it. The real creature! Right there! And I'm letting it get away! And because of that, Gretchen will probably win the contest!*

And suddenly Annie was running. Not away from the monster. No, she was sprinting back inside the house. Running up the stairs, leaping across the shattered steps, and racing up to the second floor. To the window. To her one chance of catching the Jersey Devil and getting the solid proof she needed.

Annie scrambled out onto the ledge. The giant

cryptid was just a few feet from her face. Annie swallowed, braced herself, and then . . .

She leaped!

She hung in the air for a long moment, not sure if she would make it, not sure if she would crash to the ground below and maybe possibly *really* regret ever starting on this whole freaked-out cryptids hunt.

Her head clonked against the cryptid's knee and Annie threw her arms around its hairy legs. She got a mouthful of Jersey Devil leg hair. *Gross!*

The creature howled, flapped its wings, and shot upward. But Annie hung tight. *So . . . now what's the plan?*

The Jersey Devil flew higher and higher. Its tail whipped back and forth, and it shook its legs in a desperate attempt to knock Annie loose.

And it worked. Annie's hands slipped. She was losing her grip. And then, as the Jersey Devil continued its ascent, Annie's fingers gave way.

And she was falling, falling, falling . . .

Chapter Twelve

Snowbound

CRACK!

Annie crashed though the top branch of a huge oak tree, fell through two more branches, and then landed—*hard*—in the crook of the tree in a flurry of leaves.

Lastly, an acorn fell and clonked her on the forehead. Annie sighed. *Thanks, acorn, I needed that.*

Annie rolled over, gripping the tree—she didn't need another fall—and as she did, she heard another *crack!*

"Oh, great. That was probably my shinbone," Annie muttered.

Annie sat up and searched for the source of the noise. To her amazement, she saw it was an eggshell. And a *giant* eggshell at that. And then she realized . . .

Oh man! This must be the Jersey Devil's egg!

"No wonder it was such a jerk!" Annie exclaimed. "It was just protecting its babies! And this empty shell . . . this is proof it exists!"

Annie gently placed the eggshell inside her bag. Very slowly and very carefully she climbed down the tree. She needed to get back to Mews immediately. This eggshell would be covered in cryptid DNA!

Back in the whirlybird, Annie was placing the eggshell in a padded box to keep it safe when the monitor flashed on.

"Mr. Mews! Mr. Mews, I've found another one!" She grinned into the monitor.

"An—An—Annie—" Mews's voice was crackling and fading in and out.

Annie frowned. She pounded the monitor a few times. The video flashed and flickered then finally went black.

"Mr. Mews, I've lost you," Annie said.

"Annie? Are you there?" Mews's voice returned, but now there was no video.

"I can't see you, but I can hear you." Annie frowned. She turned up the volume.

"These blasted devices . . . Technology isn't all it's cracked up to be," Mews said. "Listen, it's imperative that you get to Tibet *immediately*. There, you'll find clues to the next cryptid."

"The final one? Okay!" Annie exclaimed.

I'm going to do it. I'm going to win the contest!

"There will be a Sherpa waiting for you. The code word is *Xanadu*. Do you understand?"

Annie trusted Mews completely, so of course she agreed. "I'm on my way!" Annie said, then she banked the whirlybird and headed for East Asia.

It was early morning when Annie arrived in Tibet, and the sun was peeking over the top of the Himalayan mountain range. Even in Mews's state-of-the-art, superspeedy whirlybird it had been a long, long flight. Annie had the temperature in the helicopter cranked up to about one hundred degrees, and her breath was fogging up the windshield. She wiped the moisture away.

Through the glass, she could see the small, snow-covered village of Bei below.

The helicopter touched down just outside the village. Annie rooted around in the back of the whirlybird, found a massive winter parka, and stepped into it. It was about three sizes too big, and it felt like she was walking around in a two-hundred-pound sleeping bag.

In town, a shop owner was hanging fish outside a small food stand. "I'm supposed to meet a guide around here," Annie said. "Any idea where I might look?"

"Check the base of the mountain path," the shop owner replied.

Annie thanked him and walked through the town. It was bustling with activity, and nobody paid her any mind. In the distance, at the base of a winding mountain path, she could just make out the silhouette of a Sherpa. The guide's back was to Annie. High above them was a beautiful Tibetan monastery built into the side of the mountain.

As Annie approached, the Sherpa said, without turning, "What's the password?"

"Xanadu," Annie replied, shouting into the roaring wind.

"Perfect," the Sherpa said. And then turned around and—

The Sherpa was actually Grimlock!

"Hello, little one," Grimlock said. "You seem to have eluded me at every possible turn. The net was quite clever, I'll admit."

"You hijacked the radio!" Annie exclaimed.

"Indeed. I do a wonderful Harold Mews impression, don't you think?"

Annie glared at Gretchen.

Gretchen continued, "I trust you left the Jersey Devil's eggshell, the Loch Ness Monster's photograph, and the Chupacabra's tooth in the helicopter?"

Oh no. Annie's heart sank.

"That look tells me all I need to know," Gretchen said, grinning wickedly.

"No! I'll never let you get—"

"Sorry, I must bid you farewell," Gretchen said.

With that, Gretchen whipped a bullhorn out from behind her back and brought it to her mouth.

"So . . . *FAREWELL!*" Gretchen screamed into the bullhorn.

Annie covered her ears. Gretchen's words were impossibly loud. The sound echoed across the mountaintops. At first, Annie didn't understand. But then she felt the ground rumble . . .

Gretchen had started an avalanche.

Gretchen disappeared in a flash—and in her place was, like, *one hundred tons* of snow and ice crashing, tumbling, and rolling toward Annie.

Annie was running, trudging as fast as her little legs would allow. But the avalanche was moving harder and faster . . .

« NEWS FLASH! »

Listen up, adventure fans! BIG news!

A source tells me that Gretchen Grimlock needs only one more piece of proof to win! That's right, she has the goods on three previously never-before-proved creatures!

Could it be true?

And—an even more important question!—have we seen the last of young Annie Perkins? Last I heard she was buried up to her neck in trouble.

We'll know more soon! Stay tuned!

Chapter Thirteen

The Scalp

The snow hit Annie like a ton of bricks: enveloping her, wrapping her up, and carrying her down the mountain. As she tumbled end over end, Annie saw flashes of bright white amid glimpses of deep, dark black. Her head burst out from beneath the snow for just a moment and she gasped for air before being swallowed whole again.

After what felt like an ice-cold eternity, the avalanche slowed. Annie found herself in a small, dark hole in the snow. It was tight and freezing, and she needed to escape, *now!* She dug her hands into the snow and began digging, not even sure whether she was going up or down.

Her teeth chattered as her fingers burrowed and her feet kicked. *F-f-frozen bananas!*

Finally, Annie punched her way through the top of the snow. She could feel the sun high above her, warming her. She grabbed hold of the icy surface and pulled herself up and out as she inhaled long breaths of air.

Nothingness surrounded Annie on all sides—just long, white, endless plains. She took one shaky step and collapsed. She was too frozen and exhausted to walk. And then, filled with a deep cold that chilled her bones, she blacked out.

When Annie woke, it was dark. She no longer felt cold, just warmth coursing through her body. She felt peace and calm. *Oh great,* Annie thought. *Just great. This is what they call hypothermia!*

At that moment, a figure appeared in the distance: a cloaked silhouette in the moonlight.

"*And* I'm so cold I'm hallucinating," she said. "Awesome."

But she wasn't hallucinating. The cloaked figure was real. Two bare hands appeared and removed the hood, revealing the face of a monk. He had a bald head and a gentle smile. He reached down and picked up Annie.

"You're strong," Annie muttered, before blacking out again.

When Annie awoke, she was warm. But not bogus hypothermia warm—really warm! She was sitting next to a fire. She rubbed her eyes and looked around. She was in some sort of Tibetan monastery. Two statues of lions stood by the door. A long hall lined with ornamental window screens stretched out behind her. All around her, tall white candles burned. Across from Annie, clad in long red robes, sat the monk who had rescued her.

"You appear to be a long way from home," the monk said.

"I am," Annie said. And it hit her, then— just how far from home she really was. It had only been a few days since she left to enter the contest, but it felt like so much more. She pictured her family waiting for her—all of them together hoping, more than anything, that she'd return home with the prize that would save them. But Annie knew the truth. That would not happen.

She had failed.

"I just want to go home," Annie said, "and curl up in my bed and lie there until Christmas."

"But what about Gretchen Grimlock?" the monk asked. "Do you not want to win the contest?"

"How do you know about—?" Annie exclaimed. "Ugh. Are you one of her stupid agents?! That's it! I give up. Just throw me off a cliff or put me in a rocket to Mars or whatever else Grimlock was planning on doing."

The monk leaned forward and nudged the fire with a metal poker. "Oh, I'm certainly no friend of Ms. Grimlock's. I know her only because we've clashed before. She came here looking for the cryptid known as the Yeti many years ago. She should never be allowed near *any* creature."

Annie sighed. "Yeah, well—neither should I. What good am I? I had proof in my hands! I was close to winning the contest, and I let her take it all from me . . ."

The monk watched Annie, studying the deep frown on her face. "Please, come with me," the monk said at last. "I have something to show you."

"I'm not in the mood for a tour," Annie said, sounding very dejected.

"No. I wish to show you something that is quite sacred," the monk said, smiling. "And also quite gross!"

Annie rose to her feet and followed the monk down the long hall and through the open temple, past dozens of other monks, who were chanting. At the end of the hall was a small room, and at the center of the room stood a simple wooden shrine. Atop the shrine was something dark and brown—it reminded Annie of the horrible toupee her uncle Merle wore.

"What is it?" Annie whispered.

"It is the scalp of the Yeti."

"Eww! Like the Yeti's skin and hair and stuff?"

The monk nodded.

"Can I have it?" Annie exclaimed. "If I get this, maybe I still have a chance of winning the contest!"

"You cannot. Just as I did not allow Gretchen

Grimlock to take it many years ago, I cannot allow you to take it now."

Annie didn't understand. "Gretchen Grimlock? Why was she interested in the Yeti scalp years ago? She's only in the contest for the prize money."

"You are mistaken. There is more at stake than just prize money . . ."

Annie frowned.

"You will understand when you confront her," the monk said.

"I'm not confronting anyone," Annie said, shaking her head. "I'm taking the first flight out of here."

"You would give up so soon?" the monk asked.

"So soon?!" Annie exclaimed. "*So soon?!?* I was

blown out of the sky by a cannon! I've been duped by submarine captains and attacked by snarling monsters and flung from the legs of flying devils! I've fallen through floors and jumped off roofs and been swept up in giant avalanches! And *you* think I'm giving up *too soon*? More like *not soon enough*!"

The monk stood calm, unmoving, with his fingers intertwined. "I thought you believed," he said softly.

"I told Mews I believed in the unbelievable. And I still do. But that doesn't mean I want to get myself killed!"

"But do you not also believe in yourself?" the monk asked.

Annie stomped away, huffed, and spun back around. "What do you care, anyway?" she snapped.

"I do not like to see villains succeed. And that is what will happen if you do not finish what you started," the monk replied. "So I ask you again, Annie, do you believe in yourself?"

Annie was quiet for a short while as she thought about the dangers she had faced and the challenges she had overcome. And more, Annie thought about what would happen if Gretchen were allowed to prevail. No cryptid would ever be safe again! Annie knew that she, and she alone, could put a stop to the terror that was Gretchen Grimlock.

"Yes," Annie said finally. "Yes, I believe in myself."

"Then I will help you," the monk said, his eyes shining. "Tell me—did you know that the Yeti is the biological cousin of the American Bigfoot?"

"The American Bigfoot!" Annie exclaimed. "That's Mr. Mews's white whale . . . But how can you help?"

"Simple," the monk said, with a sly smile. "I know where Bigfoot lives . . ."

The whirlybird cut through the cool East Asian sky at maximum speed. "Mr. Mews," Annie exclaimed. "Mr. Mews! Come in!"

"Annie, it's me. What happened?!"

"Gretchen hijacked the radio frequency! But it's fine! She thinks she knocked me out for good. But she's wrong! I've found the location of Bigfoot!"

"Bigfoot?!" Mews exclaimed.

"Yes. It is at 46.8533° North, 121.7599° West. I'm heading there right now."

KRAKKLE! The monitor hissed and the video flashed on and off.

"What's going on?!" Mews shouted, as his image flashed in and out. Suddenly, Gretchen Grimlock's face appeared on the monitor.

"No!" Annie screamed.

"I suppose it's a good thing you're so resilient," Gretchen Grimlock snarled. "Because now I too know the location of Bigfoot! I guess it's just a question of who can get there first, eh?"

« NEWS FLASH! »

Illinois Johnson on WADV Radio—that's WADV for adventure—reporting in with BIG news! Contestants, adventurers, and fortune hunters—set your coordinates for 46.8533° North, 121.7599° West.

Why, you ask? Rumor has it, that's the location of the most legendary cryptid of them all—Bigfoot! Gretchen Grimlock and crowd favorite Annie Perkins are on their way there right now . . .

Who will get ahold of the great big hairy guy first? Whoever does is going to take a giant step toward nabbing that one million dollars!

And I don't think I have to tell you who I'm rooting for . . .

Good luck, adventurers!

Chapter Fourteen

Race!

Annie had heard the news on WADV Radio like everyone else—but unlike everyone else, the news was *about her*!

She saw the other contestants as she came over the top of the mountain peak. There must have been one hundred different vehicles! They were coming from every direction. Helicopters buzzing low below her. Planes racing past her. An airship approaching from the south; an old World War II–era fighter jet flying in from the north; a wagon train of trucks and cars from the east; speedboats and massive yachts and tiny launches from the sea to the west.

"Mr. Mews, are you seeing this?" Annie asked, in awe.

"Yes," Mews said, sitting at his command station in the museum. "I'm watching it live via satellite. You know, it reminds me of a great journey I once took with my friend Jules—"

"Not now, Mr. Mews!"

The contestants were all searching for the creature known as Bigfoot—but no one knew exactly *where* to look. The monk's coordinates had sent them to an old abandoned mining town just outside Mount Rainier National Park in Washington. But Bigfoot's *exact* location was still a mystery. He could be anywhere: hiding in a cave, shrouded beneath the huge redwoods that surrounded the town, tucked away along the river that ran nearby . . . anywhere!

Annie was flying low to the ground, skimming the tops of trees. She zoomed over Flawless Frank Gomes, who had apparently managed to get out of that tar pit. Behind her was Ervin "the Machine" Makow on his motorcycle—evidently, he had escaped Gretchen's thunderstorm.

"Gretchen will be there any moment!" Mr. Mews exclaimed.

Annie kept her eyes glued to the ground below her. *If I were Bigfoot and I didn't want anyone finding me, where would I hide?*

She whizzed past the town and out over the old abandoned mine. *Hmm. I wonder . . .*

While the other contestants combed the woods and the nooks and crannies along the river, Annie landed the whirlybird near the edge of town. She crept through the quiet old ghost town, past deserted storefronts and empty inns, until she came to the entrance to the old mine. Above it hung a sign that read, in big red letters, CLOSED.

Annie's stomach rolled—she was immediately reminded of the CLOSED sign that would soon be hanging from her family's restaurant. That was the reason she had done all of this! That was why she had come this far. And she was now so close . . .

Could the sign be a sign? she wondered.

She pried away the rotten old boards that blocked the entrance to the mine shaft.

"Annie, what's your plan?" Mews asked over the Mews communicator.

"I'm playing a hunch . . . ," Annie replied as she wrenched away the last piece of wood and entered the dark mine shaft. She flicked on her flashlight. A pitch-black tunnel wormed through the earth at a near ninety-degree angle—and at the bottom was the mine. Annie braced herself against the wall and began making her way down.

Not far in, there was a sudden flapping and whooshing as what felt like a thousand bats streaked toward her.

"Ahh!" Annie screamed, covering her face.

Bats, bats, bats, bats, bats—I hate bats.

One flew directly into Annie's face and became tangled in her hair. Its gross little bat feet brushed against her cheek, making her skin crawl.

"Blasted bloodsuckers!" she screamed. She waved at the bat, causing her to trip—and suddenly she was tumbling head over heels down the shaft.

After a long slide, she landed in a small sort of cave—she could barely make out a sign that said it was the spillway. Annie's hands searched for the flashlight in the darkness.

She felt something.

Hmm . . feels a lot furrier than a flashlight . . . Uh-oh . . .

Annie jumped back. Her foot landed on

something round and metal—her flashlight!
Quickly, she picked it up and flicked it on.

Oh my . . .

Bigfoot sat in the corner of the dark spillway.
Bigfoot was, indeed, big—a giant apelike creature,
nearly eight feet tall and covered in thick black
and brown hair. All around him were discarded
half-eaten fruits and vegetables.

Very slowly, Annie reached up and flicked on
her Mews communicator. "I'm looking at him,"
she whispered.

"Who?" Mews asked.

"Bigfoot," Annie whispered.

Annie heard Mews breathe in sharply. And,
for once, he was quiet.

"So, um, Mr. Bigfoot, look," Annie said. "I
kind of messed up. I brought a lot of people here,
looking for you. And if the wrong person gets their
hands on you, I'm not sure what will happen to
you—but it might be bad."

Bigfoot stared back at Annie blankly.

Right . . .

Annie sighed and banged her fist against the

wall. "Mr. Mews, what do we do?"

"We need to get him back here," Mews said. "Show the world he exists. And then put him in a nature preserve, where he's safe and can live free— instead of hiding away in a miserable mine shaft."

"Okay," Annie said. "Um, any ideas on how I might do that?"

Suddenly, a red light shone down the mine shaft from above.

"Little Annie Perkins," a voice called out. "Are you down there?"

Oh no, it's Grimlock . . .

Bigfoot held up his massive paws and shielded his face from the red light. Suddenly, he jumped up—and stood on two feet like a human.

"GRAWWRRR!" Bigfoot roared.

"Yikes!" Annie said, stumbling back.

The massive cryptid charged past Annie and up the mine shaft. Annie scrambled up behind him. She saw him roar past Grimlock.

"Um, Bigfoot?" Annie called after him as she ran. "Mr. Bigfoot! Stop! You don't want to go out there!"

Annie burst out into the daylight. Bigfoot was out in the open, running down the street. And once again, Grimlock had disappeared . . .

Chapter Fifteen

Get Him!

Bigfoot raced down the abandoned ghost town's small main street. Annie sprinted to the whirlybird, scrambled up and in, and in seconds she was in the air. And so was everyone else—there were so many flying machines that it looked like an air show.

"What do you see from the satellite?" Annie asked Mews.

Mews watched Bigfoot charge through the town and out toward the thick surrounding forest area. "To the east!" Mews shouted.

Annie gripped the control stick and the whirlybird swooped and turned. She spotted Bigfoot crossing a stream and nearing the woods. Annie pushed the stick forward, but it was too late—a second later, the creature disappeared into the woods.

"Bananas!" Annie exclaimed. "I lost him! The trees are too thick—I can't see anything!"

Annie pulled back on the stick, and the whirlybird climbed up into the air, giving her a wider view of the ground below. She craned her neck, looking for either Bigfoot or Gretchen, but saw nothing.

For a moment, everything was very calm. All the contestants were watching the woods, waiting for Bigfoot to appear. Annie caught her breath, and then . . .

Bigfoot burst out of the woods! He charged across a large meadow toward a narrow canyon! Everyone gave chase—planes dove, choppers banked, and trucks turned and raced.

But the massive cryptid was too quick. Mountain walls surrounded the town, and Bigfoot had spotted a narrow mountain pass. In an instant he had hurdled a large rock barrier, sprinted into the mountain pass, and disappeared from sight. Cars and trucks could follow him in there, but not Annie.

"I wonder if he'll come out the other side,"

Annie said. "That's my only chance."

Her question was answered when a purple helicopter, with the words GRIMLOCK GYRO across the side, rose up from over the small mountainside.

Oh no.

Attached to the bottom of the *Grimlock Gyro* was a heavy metal chain. Hanging from the end of that chain was a large metal cage, and inside the cage was Bigfoot.

Annie's heart sank.

The gyro cut through the air.

"Grimlock has him!" Annie said, looking down at the monitor to inform Mews—but instead of Mews, she saw Grimlock's wicked smile looking back at her! Grimlock had taken over the frequency once again. The monitor flashed back and forth between Grimlock and Mews.

"I'll never give you the prize money, Grimlock!" Mews said.

Grimlock cackled. "I don't need your silly contest! Do you know what the world will pay to see Bigfoot in a cage?! I'll be rich forever!"

Annie narrowed her eyes and threw the stick

forward, giving chase, slicing through the air behind the *Grimlock Gyro*. The cage dangled dangerously. Grimlock buzzed across treetops, and the cage banged against a giant oak and spun wildly. Bigfoot's hands clung to the bars. He looked like he was going to be sick.

I need to finish this before she gets that poor thing killed.

Gretchen flew low, and the cage dragged down a long dirt road. Gretchen was using the cage like a wrecking ball!

Vehicles careened out of the way! I. P. Lawe's patented *I. P. Interceptor* jerked to the right to avoid the cage—and drove straight into a ditch! Frank Gomes and his *Perfect Peddler* didn't last a second—the Bigfoot cage crashed into it and sent him spinning out of control. The Bandini Brothers swerved and splashed into a small river that ran alongside the road.

Gretchen took the chopper higher up into the sky. Vicki Voyager in her hydroplane dove to avoid the Bigfoot cage. A moment later, Annie looked down to see the hydroplane lying in pieces and Vicki crawling from the wreckage.

"Annie," Mews shouted, "you need to stop this now before Grimlock gets someone killed!"

Annie's mind raced. She needed to get Bigfoot free. She had one idea, but . . . *It's so crazy, it just might work.*

Annie threw the control stick back and the whirlybird climbed into the air until she was flying just above the *Grimlock Gyro*. She peered out the window at the gyro and cage below. *You are nuts, Annie Perkins. Nuts!*

Annie hit the switch marked AUTOPILOT, and then threw open the door and climbed out onto the ledge of the whirlybird.

She closed her eyes and jumped.

KA-KRASH!

Hard and loud, Annie landed atop the Bigfoot cage. The spinning gyro blades above her threatened to send her flying off—or worse . . .

Grimlock looked down and scowled. The villain jerked the stick side to side, rocking the gyro and trying to shake Annie off. But Annie wrapped her fingers around the chain that connected the cage to the helicopter and held tight.

Then, very carefully, Annie climbed to her feet while holding on to the heavy chain.

"Now, to land this thing," Annie said, as she eyed the cap to the gyro's gas tank. She shinnied up the chain, putting one hand over the next.

Grimlock flung open the gyro's door. "Don't you do it!" she screamed at Annie.

Ignoring her, Annie climbed up onto the side of the gyro and unscrewed the gas-tank cap. Gasoline gushed out, and the *Grimlock Gyro* immediately began to plummet.

Then, for the *coup de grâce*, Annie reached through the gyro's window and grabbed the evidence that Gretchen had stolen: the photo of the Loch Ness Monster, the Chupacabra tooth, and the Jersey Devil eggshell.

Gretchen's eyes went wide and her mouth hung agape. "I'll get you, Annie Perkins—that is a *promise*!"

Annie grinned and flashed Gretchen a wink, frustrating the villain even further. Then

Annie slid back down the chain, ripped off her backpack, and tied the straps to the top of the cage.

Annie released the connector on the chain and—*SNAP!*—the Bigfoot cage was released from the helicopter and plunged through the air.

Hurry, hurry, hurry! Falling fast!

Wind whipped through Annie's hair. It felt like they were falling at a thousand miles an hour! Annie held on tightly and pulled the rip cord on the side of her backpack, releasing her Mews Foundation Industrial Strength Parachute. With a *whoosh*, it burst open.

Several terrifying moments later, Annie, Bigfoot, and the cage gently touched down on the ground.

Annie looked to the sky. In the distance, she could see the *Grimlock Gyro* dropping fast, still leaking fuel.

The other contestants stood around Annie, looking on in awe. Cars were destroyed, bikes were overturned, planes and helicopters had crash-landed—all because of Gretchen Grimlock!

But now, it was over. Annie had done it. She had won.

"C'mon," she said to Bigfoot. "Let's get you someplace safe."

Chapter Sixteen

Happiness!

Mr. Mews, Annie, and Annie's entire family gathered at the Mews mansion. Annie's mom couldn't stop hugging and kissing her. Her father looked on with a huge, proud smile.

"Now what?" Annie asked.

Mews was leaning against the cage. Inside, Bigfoot was sitting on his big hairy butt and eating bananas. "I had hoped to buy up all the land around Bigfoot's natural habitat and turn it into a reserve," Mews said. "A place where he could live safely, in peace."

"That sounds like a great plan!" Annie said.

Mews frowned. "Unfortunately, I spent all my money on this contest! Once I pay you, I'll be broke!"

Annie's heart sank. She didn't know what to say. She didn't want to be the reason Bigfoot was

forced to return to the mine shaft or got stuck
living in a cage. But she had entered the contest to
save her family's business—and she had won!

Then Annie had a lightbulb of an idea!

"I'll tell you what," Annie said. "You keep
the money and build the habitat. But you
hire me to look after it! My parents can
open a new restaurant nearby, and I
can continue working with you to find
other cryptids and keep them safe
from Grimlock!"

Mews scratched his head. "Hmm. Not a bad idea . . ."

Annie looked at her mom and dad. They both smiled and nodded.

"Great!" Annie said. "So . . . what cryptid are we going to find next?"

Turn the page for a sneak preview of

available now!

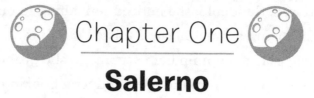

Chapter One

Salerno

NEW MESSAGE RECEIVED . . . NEW MESSAGE RECEIVED . . . NEW MESSAGE RECEIVED

The words flashed brightly across the computer monitor, but Commander Rachel Salerno was too busy to notice. Instead, she sat hunched over her workstation, poring over the mountain of notes, maps, and drawings that littered her desk.

"Where are you, Number Four?" she mumbled to herself. As the only astronaut remaining on the moon, she talked to herself a lot these days. True, the lunar facility felt quiet and lonely without the chatter of the other astronauts who had once lived and worked with Salerno, but at least there weren't any distractions now, especially when she was so close to finding what she was looking for.

"I know you're out there," she said, her brow

furrowed. Suddenly, she noticed something in one of the pictures, a detail she'd missed until now. Barely able to contain her excitement, she grabbed a page of notes from the pile of papers. Looking back and forth between her notes and the picture, she let out a gasp.

"Of course! If my calculations are correct, then Number Four must be located in the Northeast Sector! But where?" she asked, her voice echoing down the empty hall of the barracks.

As she pondered this question, she sat back in her chair and, for the first time, noticed the blinking words on the computer monitor. With a click of the mouse, she retrieved the message from her inbox. As she read, her sparkling eyes grew dark.

COMMANDER SALERNO, AGAIN AND AGAIN YOU HAVE DISOBEYED MY ORDERS. YOUR INSISTENCE ON IGNORING YOUR DUTIES AND CONTINUING THIS SILLY QUEST OF YOURS IS SIMPLY UNACCEPTABLE. AS I'VE SAID BEFORE, THIS IS NO TIME TO BE SEARCHING FOR LITTLE GREEN MEN. I AM SENDING SOMEONE TO RELIEVE YOU AND BRING YOU BACK TO EARTH. YOU

ARE ADVISED TO GATHER YOUR BELONGINGS AND
PREPARE FOR YOUR RETURN HOME.

–ROGER MCNABB, DIRECTOR OF THE
POPTROPICA ACADEMY OF SPACE EXPLORATION

"So, McNabb's sending someone to get me, is he? I'm on a 'silly quest,' am I?" Salerno put her face in her hands, feeling much like a cornered animal. For a moment she sat still, weighing her few options. At last she sat up straight and looked defiantly at the message on the computer screen, as though she was looking at McNabb himself. "No, McNabb, you can't stop me now, not when I'm so close to finding Number Four!"

And with this, she left her workstation and began making preparations for her escape.

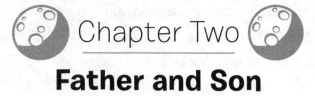

Chapter Two

Father and Son

Back on Earth, Glen Johns struggled to keep up with his father as they walked across the parking lot toward Cape Carpenter. Mr. Johns could barely keep himself from sprinting to the space center's entrance.

"Gosh, this is exciting, isn't it, Glen?" said Mr. Johns, who was huffing and puffing from the brisk pace. "To think that we're here to see the very last space launch is just amazing!"

Glen didn't say anything. He was tired from the long car ride and feeling a little cranky. Plus, he hadn't really wanted to come to Cape Carpenter in the first place.

"It's not every day you get to be a part of—"

"History. I know, Dad," said Glen. "You already said that, like, ten times in the car."

Mr. Johns chuckled. "Well, it's true. They're

shutting down the space program after this launch." After a pause he added quietly, "It's sad, really, but at least we're here to say good-bye."

Glen heard his father but, again, didn't reply. Instead, he eyed the rocket off in the distance. It looked very small sitting on its launchpad hundreds of yards away. But Glen knew that it was enormous. The first time he and his dad came to watch a launch, he was only four years old. The rocket was the biggest, most exciting thing Glen had ever seen. "Faster, Daddy," Glen had said as they raced across the parking lot, holding hands.

But Glen was thirteen years old now. He no longer needed to hold his father's hand, and he didn't really care about rockets or space travel anymore. Like dinosaurs and superheroes, space was just something he'd outgrown over the years. As he walked, he looked at the excitement on his father's face and wondered how a grown-up could care so much about something so silly.

"Yeah," said Mr. Johns, "it's hard to believe that there will be no more space launches after today. What a shame."

"Dad, if you think the space program is so important, why are they shutting it down?" Glen asked.

The question stung Mr. Johns a bit. He knew that his son was no longer a little boy and that he'd become interested in other things. Still, hearing Glen say "if *you* think it's so important" made him a little sad. He remembered the days when they both thought that space travel was important and looked forward to their special days together at Cape Carpenter. Inside, Mr. Johns had hoped for just one more of those special days.

"Well," replied Mr. Johns, "I guess most people don't care about space travel the way they used to. And since the people aren't interested anymore, the government decided to spend its money on other things."

"Well, maybe the people are right," Glen said. "I mean, what's the point of going into space?"

"To explore!" Mr. Johns replied. "Think back to the days of Christopher Columbus and the other great explorers. What they all had in common was the desire to know what's out there,

to discover their world."

Glen frowned and said, "I don't know, Dad, it seems like we've pretty much discovered all there is to find."

Mr. Johns smiled, thinking back to the days when Glen would stay up way past his bedtime, asking question after question about the moon, the stars, and the planets of the galaxy. Back then, the boy was filled with so much wonder, so much curiosity. At last, Mr. Johns said, "Son, the universe is a mighty big place. It seems to me that it'd be a shame if we ever stopped exploring it."

Glen resisted the urge to roll his eyes, but he couldn't help himself from muttering, "Space travel might have been cool, like, a million years ago, but maybe it's time to accept that things have changed."

Yes, they certainly have, Mr. Johns thought. *And it doesn't look like they'll ever be the way they were.*

Father and son walked the rest of the way in silence, until they reached the entrance to Cape Carpenter.

Chapter Three

Cape Carpenter

"Where is everyone?" said Mr. Johns in astonishment as he passed through the gates to Cape Carpenter's outdoor promenade. In years past, it would have been filled with hundreds, even thousands, of space enthusiasts on launch days. Today, though, there was only a small group of people milling about. The crowd was so small, in fact, that Mr. Johns wondered if he had the day of the launch wrong. He approached a man handing out brochures, assuming he'd have some answers.

"Excuse me, sir," said Mr. Johns, "today is the day of the launch, isn't it?"

"Indeed, it is," replied the man. "And once they wrap up this last little mission, construction will begin on Cosmic Condos."

"Cosmic Condos?"

"That's right," said the man. "All these

buildings you see here will be torn down, and in their place will be the most luxurious, most modern apartment buildings you've ever seen. Here, why don't you take one of these brochures and consider purchasing—"

"No, thanks," said Mr. Johns. "We're just here to watch the launch." As he and Glen walked on, he said, "I can't believe they're replacing all this with condos! It's bad enough that the space program is closing down, but this is a historical landmark. Do they really have to take that away, too?"

Glen was tempted to repeat what he'd already said about changing times, but he saw that his dad was a little shaken and decided to keep quiet.

"Well," Mr. Johns said with a weak laugh, "at least we're here on the right day." Then he saw something that seemed to brighten his spirits. "Glen, look! It's Captain Gordon!"

Sitting at a small table behind a sign that said MEET A REAL ASTRONAUT was a silver-haired man of about eighty years. He was there to sign autographs, but since no one was in line, he killed time with a crossword puzzle.

"Captain Gordon?" Glen asked. "Who's that?"

"Don't you remember?" Mr. Johns replied. "Deke Gordon was once one of the biggest names in space exploration, a real hero! Why, if it wasn't for him, we wouldn't know the first thing about how weightlessness affects hamster behavior! Come on, let's go meet him."

Glen didn't recognize the name, but he followed his father, who was already approaching the man.

"Captain Gordon, this sure is a treat," Mr. Johns said to the retired astronaut.

"Well!" replied Gordon, putting down his puzzle. "It's nice to be remembered by *someone*. You're the first person to actually recognize me. The only other person I talked to just stopped by to ask me if Cape Carpenter still sells those rocket-shaped ice pops."

"Are you kidding?" Mr. Johns said, his hands shaking with excitement. "I idolized you as a kid. I had a poster in my bedroom of you walking on the moon!"

"Yes, those were some great days," Captain Gordon said with a laugh. "But they happened long, long ago, I'm afraid." Pointing at a picture on the table, he added, "It's hard to believe that this man and I are the same person." Glen and Mr. Johns looked at the picture, which showed a much younger Captain Gordon riding on the back of a convertible, as thousands of parade-goers cheered him on.

"I remember that," Mr. Johns said. "That was right after you returned from building the first lunar facility on the moon!"

"You have a good memory," Captain Gordon said, smiling. "Yes, back in those days, people couldn't get enough of space exploration. We astronauts were like rock stars!" Then, his smile fading, he added, "But as you can see, things have changed."

Glen had been listening quietly, but he understood what Captain Gordon meant. Hardly anyone had come to watch the launch, and no one cared about meeting some retired astronaut.

"Captain Gordon," said Mr. Johns, looking to

brighten the mood, "this is my son, Glen. He and I have been to half a dozen space launches."

"It's nice to meet you, Glen," said Captain Gordon. "I'm happy to see that there are some young people who still have an interest in space exploration."

Glen's face reddened. He didn't have the heart to tell Captain Gordon that he wasn't really interested in space anymore, or that he would rather be at home watching television. Instead, he just shook the astronaut's hand.

"Glen," Mr. Johns said, "do you have any questions you'd like to ask Captain Gordon?" The boy blushed even more. "Uh," he said, looking down at his feet. "*Do* they still sell those rocket-shaped ice pops here?"

Captain Gordon raised his eyebrows in surprise.

"Ha-ha," Mr. Johns laughed. "He's just joking. Captain Gordon, thanks so much for your time. Meeting you was a thrill!"

"The pleasure was mine," the astronaut replied. "I hope your last visit to Cape Carpenter is memorable. Enjoy the launch."

"Ice pops?" Mr. Johns said under his breath as he and Glen moved on. "That's the only thing you could think to ask?"

"I'm sorry, Dad," Glen said, feeling irritated. "I didn't know I was supposed to have a list of prepared questions."

Mr. Johns paused and collected himself. "Yeah, Glen," he said, "you're right. I shouldn't have put you on the spot like that. Hey, we still have about an hour before the launch. How about we grab something to eat and then hit the gift shop?"

Glen wasn't angry anymore, but he felt like he could use a break from his dad. "Uh, if you don't mind, I'd kind of like to walk around on my own for a while."

"Oh," Mr. Johns said, feeling like his plans for a perfect day were going south. "But I thought we were going to hang out together today."

"We have been together, Dad," Glen said. "We spent the car ride together, we'll watch the launch together, and we'll drive home together. But I'm thirteen years old; I'm not a little kid anymore. I just want to be by myself for a little while."

"Um, I guess that's okay," Mr. Johns said a little reluctantly. He'd noticed that Glen reminded him that he was thirteen a lot these days. "Here," he said, handing Glen a few dollars, "take this and let's meet up in the spectator stands in an hour."

"Okay, thanks, Dad," Glen said, taking the money. He began walking away but didn't get very far before he heard his father's voice.

"Glen," Mr. Johns called, "be careful!"

Glen didn't turn to acknowledge that he'd heard his dad. He just walked on, rolling his eyes. *Sheesh,* he thought, *it's just an hour. It's not as though I'm going to the moon.*